Snow White and the Dragon

the Princess Swap

Sleeping Beauty and the Seven Dwarfs

Don't miss any adventures in
The Princess Swap

Snow White and the Dragon

the Princess Swap

Sleeping Beauty and the Seven Dwarfs

Kim Bussing

RANDOM HOUSE · NEW YORK

Text copyright © 2025 by Penguin Random House LLC
Cover art copyright © 2025 by Sara Lozoya

Visit us on the Web! rhcbooks.com

Educators and librarians, for a variety of teaching tools, visit us at RHTeachersLibrarians.com

Library of Congress Cataloging-in-Publication Data is available upon request.
ISBN 978-0-593-70807-1 (hc)—ISBN 978-0-593-70808-8 (lib. bdg.)—
ISBN 978-0-593-70806-4 (pbk.)—ISBN 978-0-593-70809-5 (ebook)

The text of this book is set in 12-point Garamond Classico and P22 Franklin Caslon.
Old paper texture by releon8211/stock.adobe.com
Vintage vector border by Extezy/stock.adobe.com

Editor: Tricia Lin
Cover Designer: Michelle Cunningham
Interior Designer: Michelle Canoni
Copy Editor: Barbara Bakowski
Managing Editor: Rebecca Vitkus
Production Manager: Tracy Heydweiller

Printed in the United States of America
10 9 8 7 6 5 4 3 2 1
First Edition

Random House Children's Books supports the First Amendment and celebrates the right to read.

To Dad and Jen,

for the video games, hikes beneath the evergreens,
and encouraging me to pursue the big things

O nce upon a time, a princess's heart turned to stone.

No, sorry. We're not there yet.

Let's start over.

Once upon a time, two princesses betrayed each other for a crown—

No. Now we're starting too early.

But pay attention. Fortune favors those who can see things for what they really are.

We'll begin here instead:

Once upon a time, there was a queen who went hunting for a curse.

She came from a long line of queens who had a history of untangling, breaking, and, on rare occasions, casting curses.

But the history books will tell you that she found herself pregnant with no curse necessary. After all, there are certain things you want to keep away from history's eyes.

The impending princess's birth was a cause for celebration. A single princess was always born in this kingdom, to one day take over the throne, and it had been that way for centuries upon centuries, and centuries before that.

Of course, no other queen needed to resort to curses in order to have a child. No other queen had tried, year after year, to conceive a child, only to watch the royal nursery remain empty. That made this queen quite desperate.

Before the princess's arrival, the kingdom's people gossiped about the color of her hair: Would it be black, like her mother's and like the kingdom's First Queen's? Or half copper, half gold, as a queen's was every century or so, the same as the First Queen's wicked sister's?

While they picked up their bread at the baker's, they debated what the princess's birth might mean for their taxes.

At the pub at night, they wondered what fairy blessings the new princess might receive.

In this kingdom, magic always lurked close at hand. It sprouted from the soil and would stain your fingertips, and you were at risk of being zapped into a ferret if you were a little rude to a touchy banshee. And for each of Apfel's princesses, seven of Reverie's good fairies bestowed a blessing upon the child.

Perhaps you can see where this is going.

But no one else did. Instead, the entire kingdom of Apfel rejoiced. With every birth came plentiful crops and unexpected treaties between warring goblins or angry bandits. Gold coins would appear in the gutters, within loaves of bread, in the heels of shoes.

Except before *this* princess was born, gold coins crumbled into dust. Dirt roads turned to mud, even on sunny days. Pigeons refused to deliver mail. Milk curdled in the pails, bread hardened to iron, and pillows vanished from beneath people's heads halfway through the night.

Taken alone, these could each mean plenty of things.

But few saw how the queen's belly grew larger and larger as she fell sicker and sicker, how the paintings of the past queens lost their smiles. In the castle's courtyard, two apple trees bloomed year-round, one with red blossoms and the other with flowers as pearly as snow. But now none appeared on the branches, and all the leaves fell to the ground.

The king and queen worked to ensure that no one thought *curse*. The queen had not meant for this to happen. She didn't realize what she had offered to give up.

So the royal family ordered gold platters for the feast, and the chefs worked without sleep for three days. Artists calligraphed the invitations. Outside, storms began.

You know what comes next, don't you?

After midnight but before dawn, a baby girl was

born, with skin white as snow, lips red as a rose, and hair black as a raven's wing. And the queen grew weaker.

Seven of the land's most respected and powerful fairies were invited to the feast. As rain and wind rattled the windows, the fairies drank from goblets of diamond alongside the king; they feasted on honey cakes; and, as was the custom, they met alone with the fading queen and the child. They each bestowed a gift upon the young princess: honesty from the Fairy of Grace, beauty from the Fairy of Joy, generosity from the Fairy of Breadcrumbs, a lovely voice from the Fairy of Singing Canaries, sweet dreams from the Fairy of the North Star, a backbone from the Fairy of Hummingbirds, who was getting a bit fed up with gifts she thought made a girl too submissive. But before the Fairy of Flora could bestow her gift, the storm worsened.

Glass shattered in windows. Torches guttered out. Hats turned into live birds and fluttered away.

Lightning flurried, bringing with it a very cruel witch, terribly displeased to find that despite her role in bringing the princess into being, she had not received an invitation.

Rumors swirled that she was the evil sister of Apfel's First Queen, seeking revenge throughout all the centuries. But she offered such dazzling promises of love, glory, and riches that even those who knew better took the risk of bargaining with her.

The queen should have known better.

The witch's face was hidden beneath a black veil; her dress looked like it was made out of onyx scales. Like the fairies, she bestowed her gift upon the child in private, where only the ailing queen could hear.

It was no blessing, but a curse. On her thirteenth birthday, the princess would fall into an eternal sleep.

And so would everyone else.

Don't believe everything you hear.

After all, nobody ever talks about how the princess vanished that night. Nobody ever talks about how seven good fairies entered the throne room's doors and only six left.

But that's because, according to everyone, that never happened.

1

Snow

IT'S OVER.

It's always over.

Sometimes Snow just gets a little farther.

"This section of the city's closed to the public, miss."

Two guards pace forward, dawn glancing off the heavy plated helmets.

"Fine," Snow declares, stuffing the paper bag within her cloak so they won't see it. "I'll go the other way."

This part of the city isn't usually closed—it's one of Snow's favorite shortcuts—but what's more important than arguing is making sure the guards don't recognize her. She'll take any route as long as the queen doesn't hear where she is.

Well. Temporary queen.

"Hang on a moment," the guard says slowly. "I know who you are."

Snow's seen the guards not notice a family of small gnomes stealing an entire suckling pig from a market stand. If only they could be as equally unobservant today.

"You probably don't," Snow tries.

"It's her," one mutters. His eyes widen. "It is you, isn't it?"

"The streets aren't very safe for a young lady to walk alone," the other insists. She'll call him Captain Boot Licker. "Especially a certain young lady."

Snow pinches the inside of her elbow to remind herself not to make a face that would get her into more trouble.

"The streets are *very* safe," she says. "Unless you two haven't been doing your job?"

"We do our jobs," Boot Licker promises.

Snow tugs her hood tighter over her black waves. Her stepmother has been very strict about Snow not leaving the castle, and Snow would prefer that her stepmother think she's dutifully obedient. It might be a hard sell at this point, but Snow's never one to give up. She's also not given up being disobedient when the mood strikes.

She whistles, a quiet song that she can't remember where she learned but has known her entire life.

"What are you doing?" one of the guards says suspiciously.

"Be nicer," the other guard scolds. "It might be *her.*"

But before they can continue to debate who Snow may

or may not be, there's a rustling of wings and a shadow blots out the sun.

"Wha—"

A large winged thing streaks across the sky, launching itself at the guards. They shriek, scrambling away.

"Attack!" one screams. "We're under attack!"

In the commotion, Snow darts to the bustling High Street, where it's easy to get lost in the crowds. Despite what the guards think, out of all the cities in Reverie, Apfel is the safest, as long as you stick to the right neighborhoods.

Like Reverie's other five capital cities, it shares the same name as its kingdom; but unlike the others, it's plopped straight in the middle of the Dreamwood, with no walls around it. Warlocks dine at cafés, next to ogresses sipping tea and teacup-sized pixies seated on sugar cubes. Wood nymphs lead art classes in the parks; famous fairies attend local balls if the costume theme is interesting enough.

In capital cities like Miravale and Coralon, the worst a pickpocket might face is a night in jail. In Apfel, picking the wrong pocket could get you turned to stone by an annoyed witch. Risks like that encourage better behavior.

As Snow trots up the narrow road winding to the castle, the shadowy shape streaks across the sky again. Snow grins. The raven lands on her shoulder, nuzzling Snow's hair.

"Good job, Newton," she says, stroking the bird's back.

Apfel Castle sits high on a hill, its white spires topped with steep blue roofs, and the path to get there is crowded, especially at this time of year, when the trees are brilliant with red and gold leaves. Some people come here on royal business or to tour the castle, but most come for the view: the Dreamwood cascading around them, which doesn't seem so dangerous from here. The large lake at the base of the hill is dotted with a few swans. From this far away, they look like white flowers.

In the main courtyard, vendors roast candied nuts for the tourists; the nobles, wrapped in furs, hurry between buildings. A woman sings for alms near the small chapel. Keeping her head ducked down, Snow drops whatever coins she has into the woman's tin.

Snow yanks off the cloak's hood. She inhales the smell of sugared almonds. Maybe she could sneak a few. . . .

"Princess!" a noblewoman exclaims, and curtsies, and Snow smiles tightly as she rushes past.

"Princess!" a young servant girl murmurs, curtsying.

"Princess!" a merchant lord smirks, bowing.

The odd part about being a princess is that everyone knows you and talks about you, but you don't know most of them. She thought she would get over it as she got older, but it only feels stranger. And a little lonelier.

"Princess."

This time Snow stops short, and Newton takes off, a black streak winding through the castle to Snow's quarters.

Amalia folds her arms over her chest. She's not dressed for the cold, like she's daring it to try to bother her. "It's not seemly for a princess to be seen dashing around."

Amalia is Queen Consort Lucille's damafrau. When

Snow becomes queen, she'll be Snow's. Amalia is the queen's right hand, assisting with affairs of state and enforcing court policies; she's been here as long as Snow's been alive. And no matter what Snow does, Amalia treats her only with annoyance. "I'm not dashing," Snow says. "Maybe you're just . . . moving too slowly." Amalia doesn't seem amused. She never does. She has the same sense of humor as a block of iron, which she somewhat resembles, from her metal-colored curls to her rigid dresses and her terrible clogs, which make an echoing clop-clop-clop. At least they warn you when she's coming.

"Be careful, Princess," Amalia says with a slight bow. "Not everyone can be charmed by sharp words."

"Then I'll make sure to be exceptionally dull with you," Snow says as she retreats.

Apfel Castle was designed by a man who created sets for operas, and it feels just that grandiose: the wooden walls are hand-carved with the shapes of plants, columns are lined with gold, chandeliers drip with countless crystals and eternal flames.

Snow hurries to her father's chambers. He's set to head out this afternoon to make visits across their kingdom, and Snow pats the pastry bag, pleased with herself. There's a small bakery in the Old Quarter that Snow and her father both love. Her mother, Elora, loved it, too, so they say. Her mother died two days after Snow was born, and all she has is everyone else's stories.

Snow isn't entirely sure why her father has to leave in

the week leading up to the most important day of her life, but he promised to return by her Crown Ceremony, a day that makes her slightly sick to think about. When her father will place the crown of Apfel on her head for the first time, and the ghost of all the past queens will decide if she's worthy of joining their ranks. When the magic of the bloodline will flow stronger through her veins, instead of just letting her talk to the odd pigeon or Newton.

"Your ceremony? That's something I wouldn't miss, little one," he said, ruffling her hair the way you might pet a nice-looking dog. "My girl, all grown-up."

Hardly. She's only on the cusp of thirteen, still five years of training away from officially taking the throne. Snow's not *ready* to be all grown-up. Too much responsibility and paperwork.

Snow dodges secretaries and a lost-looking merchant as she reaches her father's office.

"Father." Snow opens the cracked door with her foot and holds out the slightly smooshed bag of pastries. It's emptier than when she bought the buns, but she had given some to a pair of ogre younglings. "Before you go, I thought it might—"

"He's already gone." Lucille looks up from Snow's father's desk, brushing a strand of blond hair from her forehead with the tip of a quill. "I'm afraid you've *just* missed him."

At first glance, the queen consort, Snow's stepmother, is the image of goodness. She has long, shiny golden hair, skin smooth as marble, golden eyes that are as large as coins and framed by thick lashes.

But Snow has had more than a first glance for the three years Lucille and her father have been married.

Odd things happen around Lucille, Snow is sure of it. Blazes erupt in hearths. Candles extinguish themselves. Snow's confident she caught Lucille standing close to a spiderweb, like she was reading messages left within it.

And Snow has overheard the chambermaids whispering about how they've found Lucille in the throne room, staring at the crown. It's hard for Snow to ignore the stories of all those other stepmothers, plotting, plotting, plotting.

But Snow has few people to tell her suspicions to. Lucille is, unfortunately, very well liked. She knows the names of people's babies, sends leftover food to the orphanages. It's such an obvious front that Snow's shocked no one else can see through it.

"I was looking for Father," Snow says stubbornly. "Did he leave a note?"

"What's that you have in your hand, darling?"

"Oh." Snow stares blankly at the bag. "I, um . . . I had these delivered?"

Snow not leaving the castle is one of Lucille's favorite rules, along with making her run laps and forbidding her to wander the halls after dark. But Snow is a princess, not an egg, and she's pretty positive she won't shatter.

"Snow," Lucille says slowly. "You didn't happen to be *out* of the castle this morning, did you?"

Snow was hopeful about having a mother. She liked the idea of someone to brush her hair and braid it at night, someone who wasn't a chambermaid afraid to talk to the princess. Someone who would tell her about what's it like to fall in love and get your heart broken, someone who knew how to ease blisters from wearing slippers and make the searing eyes of the world seem less . . . searing.

But most people, it turns out, just disappoint you.

Her father spends much of his time throughout Reverie on Very Important Duties of State, sampling the ale at this township or the cider in this village, charming nobles in their whiskey cellars, and returning home shrouded in the fumes of sweet wine.

And Lucille is . . . The stories of evil stepmothers have to come from somewhere, don't they?

"What are you doing at my father's desk?" Snow demands.

"I thought I told you, Snow, that you weren't to leave the castle." Lucille stands, ignoring the question. Her silky gown swirls about her, along with the smell of honeysuckle and smoke.

"Did you?" Snow scrunches her nose. "I'll remember next time."

"You're right. You will." Lucille snaps her fingers. Two guards appear at the door. "And it wouldn't be fair if, as your stepmother, I didn't give you a little bit of help."

"What are you—"

"Helping," Lucille says, smiling like they're having a

pleasant conversation. "Since staying put seems to be such a difficult concept."

The guards stride forward and grab Snow by the forearms.

"What are you *doing*?" Snow yelps. "Put. Me. Down."

"As I am queen consort and the most powerful person in this castle for the next seven days, you will listen to me," Lucille commands. She strides forward and plucks the pastries from Snow.

"Those are mine!" Snow protests. She'd been looking forward to the sugar buns.

"Take the princess to her room," Lucille declares.

"Don't take the princess to her room!" Snow exclaims. "Ex*cuse* me!"

But the guards don't listen, half-dragging and half-carrying her through private corridors to her quarters, Lucille trailing behind.

Snow's room is halfway up a tower near the back of the castle. It overlooks a small garden her mother had tended to before she—well, before she became Snow's mother and died for it.

Newton waits on Snow's writing desk, picking at crumbs from last night's half-eaten rolls. He eyes Snow strung between the guards.

The guards release her, guiding her so gently into her chambers that Snow's tempted to run past them. But there's no point. They'll catch her.

"You must understand that this is for your own good,"

Lucille simpers. "I've told you so many times, darling, that there are people out there who want to hurt you."

"I can take care of myself," Snow protests. And she was at a bakery. It wasn't like someone was going to attack her with a croissant.

"Of course you can," Lucille purrs. "But I'm here to *protect* you."

Snow scoffs. "I don't need protection."

To prove it, Snow has developed rough edges, a sharp tongue. Because they all think she's weak. And she'll do anything to keep them from thinking her worst fear: that she's not cut out to be queen.

"Perhaps not. But here we are." Lucille's voice is soft. "Didn't you hear what happened in the city this morning?"

"What?" Snow's annoyed that she's curious, but Lucille always does this, dangling little scraps to get Snow to beg for answers.

"Something terrible," Lucille says. She rests her hand on the door. "Something . . . disastrous."

That was why the section of the city was closed? Something actually happened down there?

"What?" Snow presses. Was it an attack? A sorcerer who let loose a rogue spell? A troll who no longer felt like letting people pass over his bridge peacefully?

"Rumors of the Night Witch. How terrible if she got her hands on you."

"Wouldn't you like that?" Snow mutters. With Snow

out of the way, Lucille could take the throne. But the Night Witch is long gone; Snow's not scared of rumors.

Lucille just smiles.

Too late, Snow realizes what her stepmother is about to do.

"No!" she cries, darting forward, but the heavy door swings shut.

"I'll have the kitchen send up a quiche," Lucille calls through the door, as though Snow's going to let herself be a little caged bird if she's fed breakfast.

The lock falls heavily into place.

Snow is trapped.

2

Rose

AS FAR AS ROSE IS CONCERNED, IT'S A
little early for problems.

Cross-legged on the floor of the storage room,
she hunches over the mortar and pestle. Her toxic nettles
are hissing, her dragon's bane is letting out puffs of smoke,
one pesky nightshade keeps floating in the air and nip-
ping at Rose's ears, and the potion is a puke green when
it's meant to be violet. Nothing is going the way it should.

"Rosie! There's someone—" The door swings open,
and here's another problem.

Edel stands in a fog of flour and sugar and lemon zest.
"What are you— I told you, you aren't to use those."

"It's nothing!" Rose protests. "I'm just—"

"Those aren't safe!" Edel scolds, but she can't hide a small smile at seeing what Rose is brewing. A Dreamweaver's Draught. A very tricky potion, but Rose is determined.

"I'm being careful," Rose promises. Edel worries too much. Rose has never had an issue with the more dangerous flora—sometimes she even finds them easier to work with than marigolds and baby's breath, staples in Edel's Wishes.

"Well . . . I . . . Knock off this nonsense. And come say hello." Edel sweeps some of the dragon's bane and nightshade into her fists and tucks them into her apron. Flowers as alive as these only grow in the most magical of places. "Impressive," she mutters.

With her tufts of white hair sticking out at wild angles and lemon curd splattered on her dress, Edel doesn't look like one of Reverie's most powerful fairies. But, after all, if you are that powerful, it's often better if most people don't notice.

"I'm practicing!" Rose protests, adjusting her belt bag around her waist and trailing Edel into the main room. "Will you give those back later?"

"Practicing for what?" Klaus Mertleroot asks. Everything about the head of the Western warlocks is extra long, from his height to his burlap-colored beard to his stretched-out fingers, which are currently tearing still-steaming sourdough bread.

Rose hides her surprise. Visitors turning up at their kitchen table is nothing new. The woodcutter's cottage, deep in the Dreamwood, is where Wishes are answered, and it has a reputation among magical folk as where you go to find a serum for a nasty wound, or a warm place to wait out a storm. But Klaus and the other head warlocks are supposed to be in Miravale right now, investigating that kingdom's nasty curse business.

"The Royal Apfel Academy," Rose says, fiddling with the end of her strawberry blond braid. "They're inviting new students to apply."

Edel puts a pot of tea down on the table, kissing Rose's forehead as she passes. A fire crackles merrily in the fireplace, and Klaus's goats, which he never goes anywhere without, rest on the plush sofas, occasionally nibbling on a pillow.

"Dunsectnudentryeir?" Klaus mumbles around a large bite of bread.

"Excuse me?" Edel asks.

He swallows. "Don't they accept new students every year?"

"They do," Edel agrees before Rose can speak, a protest ready on her tongue.

The RAA *does* accept new students every year, but only from within Apfel and only students who can pay the full tuition. Out-of-city and scholarship students can apply once every three years. The next time Rose can apply, she'll be *nearly sixteen*. She'll be ancient. Besides, competition to get into the RAA's School of Potion Brewing is steep.

"Why would you need some silly school when you have the best teacher right here?" Klaus gestures at Edel with a hunk of bread.

"Exactly my point," Edel says, returning to a large lemon-scented dough on a stone counter.

Edel is revered throughout Reverie, or so folk remind

Rose. Edel gets stacks of invitations addressed to the Fairy of Flora, imploring her to attend balls and royal galas, though she just ends up using them in the compost, muttering about a bad experience at a party years ago.

"It's not silly," Rose defends. "And we talked about this, Aunt Edel. You *said* when I turn thirteen, maybe I can go."

Why does she want to go? Rose has countless reasons:

1) Starting with the magical elephant in the room: Rose is a human. And aside from the Villeneuve Trading Company girl and Dimitri, hardly any kids pass through this part of the Dreamwood. Rose would like to meet people her own age.

2) She'd get to see more of the world beyond the cottage and some of the Dreamwood.

3) Edel might be the best at making uppercase Wishes—potions and tinctures and serums that fulfill people's lowercase wishes—but, once again, she's a fairy. Rose is not.

4) And not that Rose wants to get her hopes up, but Edel said she found her near Apfel as a baby. If Rose were to get into the RAA . . . if she were to encounter any family she might have left in Apfel . . . well, they couldn't exactly turn her away if she became so accomplished, could they?

But Rose doesn't say any of this, because she doesn't want to hurt Edel's feelings. Edel is the closest thing she has to a mother, and she's given Rose as much as she can. It's not Edel's fault that part of Rose yearns for a life that Edel can't create.

"And you're not yet thirteen," Edel retorts. She turns back to Klaus. "Do you need something? Is something wrong with Miravale's princess?"

"Oh, I wouldn't know," Klaus shrugs. "The princess went off with some merchants."

"She did? Princess Anisa?" Rose leans forward. Edel usually ignores human affairs, but Rose hungers for whatever news she can get. How wonderful to be a princess. To know exactly where you belong, and to have so many friends and places to go and things to do . . .

"Surely, that kind of news can be sent in a letter," Edel suggests.

"That's not the news," he says. "This isn't— This is something . . ." Klaus rises, suddenly somber. He yanks the curtains over the windows, peeks out the door before locking it tight. He even glances up the fireplace like something might be lurking there, listening.

"It's something what?" Rose presses.

"Something *bad*."

Edel clucks her tongue against her teeth. "Klaus, this is life. There's always something bad and, just as quickly, something equally good."

"We were called away from Miravale," Klaus interrupts. "Because of a curse."

"The curse was in Miravale," Edel reminds him.

"Another one."

"I haven't heard of another," Edel says mildly.

"They don't want word to spread," he says. "They say . . . they say it could be the Night Witch."

Rose knows that name. The Night Witch cast a sleeping curse centuries ago, in Apfel. Folk in the Dreamwood have been muttering about her recently, but they aren't that concerned. There are worse things in the Wood.

"People will say anything, won't they?" But Edel's voice is a little bit too high. Her hands shake as she sips her tea.

Edel's hands never shake.

"Why do people care about the Night Witch?" Rose leans forward so far that the tip of her braid nearly falls into her cup. Her interest is piqued. What could make *Edel* so nervous?

Klaus freezes, his mouth half open. "You don't—"

Edel's hands tremble so badly that dark tea spills over the tree trunk table. "It sounds as though there's a lot on your plate," she says. "You should be going, Klaus."

"What?" Rose demands. "What were you going to say, Klaus?"

"Edel . . . ," Klaus begins.

"Klaus," Edel interrupts, her gaze fiery.

"They're falling asleep!" Klaus bursts out. "There are rumors of shepherds just outside Apfel, all fallen asleep, and you're not going to say anything? What good does silence do, Edel?"

"It silences unnecessary panic," Edel shoots back, tea spilling again as she tries to drink.

"Asleep?" Rose asks. "People are falling asleep? What? How? *Why?*"

The silence stretches like taffy. One of the goats bleats. Klaus mutters something under his breath and goes back to the fireplace, peering so far into the chimney that the tip of his long nose is stained with soot.

"We've said too much already," he says. "But it was safer than a letter."

People falling asleep doesn't seem like that big a deal. That's . . . kind of what people do.

So Rose doesn't need to be worried. It probably won't impact her application to the RAA.

She can think that as much as she likes, but it doesn't explain Edel's response. It doesn't explain why Klaus is hunting for spies in the chimney. If this is just a matter of waking them up, Edel can spin up an alertness Wish in less than an hour. Or they could try stronger coffee.

"We'll see you for Rosie's birthday?" Edel asks, her voice tight. She gestures toward a corner of the kitchen packed with tottering bags of flour, sugar, cocoa powder, coconut flakes, and sprinkles imported from Ambrosia. "Thirteen cakes for her thirteenth."

"Wouldn't miss it." He pats the top of Rose's head.

He gathers his goats and is out the door before Rose's mind can stop spinning with curses, and fairies, and exhausted shepherds.

"Why does it matter if people are falling asleep?" Rose asks.

Edel shoves the lemon bread dough into the clay oven, then wipes her floured hands on her apron. "Lavender. You forgot it in your draught," Edel says. "If you're going to attempt a Dreamweaver's Draught without my supervision, don't forget a sprig of lavender."

Rose takes this as an opening to bring up the RAA again—after all, if people in Reverie are extraordinarily tired, wouldn't it be helpful if more alchemists knew how to brew potions and elixirs to help?

"For the application . . ."

Edel interrupts: "The Huntsmen will be stopping by short—"

The door slams open. Klaus bustles back into the cottage, pausing as Edel rounds on him, looking horrified. "I couldn't not say anything," he says. "You best be careful, Rosie girl."

"Why?" Rose asks. The tiniest bit of concern prickles at the back of her mind.

"Klaus," Edel warns. "What you were told, you were told in confidence. Poorly placed confidence, clearly. Certain things are better not said."

He ignores her. "This is what they said would happen. That it would start slow. But no one would be safe. *Everyone* in Apfel would be cursed into an unwaking sleep."

"*Klaus,*" Edel interrupts, her gaze fiery.

He ignores her. "The exact same curse that is coming for you, Rose."

3

Snow

SNOW HURLS HER FOOT AT THE HEAVY DOOR, expecting the triumphant moment where her fierce strength shatters the lock—but instead she reels back, grimacing and hopping in place as her toes sting.

"How are you supposed to take your throne if you cannot even walk to it?"

Leaning against her writing desk, petting Newton, stands a man half Snow's height, his curly blond hair pulled back in a ponytail. Like the other star-reading dwarfs, magical creatures that have long lived and worked closely with humans, he wears a jumpsuit made out of eucalyptus leaves woven tight, a tradition passed down from mining dwarfs for safety within the tunnels. His is dyed red.

"Bootes!" Snow exclaims. "How did . . . ?"

"The stars told me you might need a hand," Bootes says. He gestures toward a wall that's no longer a wall, revealing a slim entranceway. Beyond it is a series of passages that run the whole of the castle, lit by salt lamps. They were built when the castle was, as a safety measure imposed by the First Queen. Once, Snow tried to navigate the tunnels alone; she thought she was at her bedroom but instead found herself walking into a sauna full of visiting ambassadors. It wasn't fun for anyone.

Snow follows Bootes through the dim corridor as she frustratedly recounts what Lucille did.

"Aren't we going up?" Snow asks. They usually climb high; today, they go down, and Bootes pauses in front of a stretch of wall.

At the top of the castle's tallest tower sits the Astratorium, entered only by Bootes and the six other dwarfs as they read the prophecies and warnings spoken by the stars.

Just below that is the dwarfs' dormitory, where everything is found in sevens and Snow has spent a decent amount of her time, especially since Lucille arrived. No one supposes the princess is with the dwarfs, who are known to be stoic and solitary. No one supposes they give her wild-mushroom sourdough and let her spend her free hours by the crackling warmth of their potbellied stove, one of the places in the world where she's happiest. Where she can just be *Snow*.

"Not today, little one," Bootes says. "The stars . . . have much to say."

"You're still working?" Usually the dwarfs go to sleep once dawn peeks over the horizon.

But Lucille said something happened in the city today. . . .

Nothing ever happens to Snow, and she knows this is probably serious, though she's so curious she feels like she could hop up and down. But princesses aren't supposed to be excitable.

"Is something going on, Bootes? You have to tell me. *Pleeeeease.*"

Bootes slides the wall open, revealing a hallway near the kitchens. Pots clang, the chef de cuisine yells, knives thump on cutting boards, delicious smells waft through the air.

"You should hurry," Bootes says. "You will still be able to make breakfast. And do not tell Orion about this. I was not supposed to come rescue you."

You'll never get the answers you want if you try to argue with a dwarf, so Snow thanks him and retreats into the hallway, cheered at the thought of Lucille seeing her free, and the freedom of not having guards trailing her—

"Princess. What an unexpected surprise."

Snow pales as she turns around. Amalia's smile looks more like a scowl.

"That's one word for it," Snow agrees. She hadn't heard Amalia coming, the kitchen sounds drowning out the clop-clop-clop.

"And what fortunate timing. I was hoping I'd run into you. And alone, no less."

Snow doesn't bother to hide her grimace. If the stars went through the trouble of getting Bootes to free her, they could also have warned her about where Amalia might pop up.

"I wanted to go for a walk," Snow sniffs. Amalia is Lucille's watchdog, lurking around corners to report what she deems improper, reprimanding the cooks for over-salting the cod or undersalting the steak, the florists for not including enough pink in their morning bouquets, the footmen for not tucking in their shirts properly. Snow had hoped her grand escape from the locked tower wouldn't involve Amalia tattling on her. "And now I'm late."

Amalia probably knows exactly what's on Snow's schedule. Which right now is nothing.

"Princess," Amalia repeats. "Before I served the queen consort, I served your mother. There's something you need to know."

Snow narrows her eyes.

She can't resist a secret.

"Is it about . . . my Crown Ceremony?"

Amalia nods, gesturing down another corridor. "Certain things are better said in private," she insists.

Could she be . . .

Could she be loyal to Snow, an ally that Snow hadn't realized she had?

Amalia starts off at a trot away from the kitchens, the clunking of her clogs echoing oddly down the narrow passageway.

Snow hesitates.

Amalia's always treated her with a kind of calculated disdain. But there's no harm in following her and hearing what she has to say. And it feels queenly and exciting to be alone with the damafrau, to be invited into serious discussions.

She hurries after Amalia up a flight of stairs. This part of the castle is quieter and emptier. They reach a plain door. Amalia nudges it open, and Snow gasps.

She was expecting a storage cabinet, but this room is glorious, with a vaulted ceiling soaring stories above. The wallpaper is made of raised gold thread intricately woven to look like a forest. Looking at the ceiling is like gazing up at the branches of a massive tree.

The room is mostly empty, aside from a large claw-footed mirror with very dirty glass.

"Queen Regina's ballroom," Amalia says, observing Snow out of the corner of her eye. "Your great-grandmother. She had this room built after the Seven-Year Witches War, in celebration of Lady Grimm establishing the Dreamwood Council."

"I didn't know that," Snow admits. Maybe she should be a little more curious about her family's history, but the weight of it all makes her nervous. Her grandmothers ended wars, brokered truces, defined Apfel's and Reverie's history.

It is much easier to roll her eyes and yawn than to admit that she isn't sure she can be like them. Especially when no one has ever really said that they think she can, either.

"It has always disappointed me," Amalia says, "how few of Apfel's queens have truly lived up to the precedent set by the first."

"Well. I . . . promise to do that," Snow says, fidgeting. As if. Nora, First Queen of Apfel, *created* Apfel. Snow's never even baked a cake. Late at night, when she can't sleep, she worries that she wasn't born with what makes other queens fit to be queen. That without her mother to teach her, she'll never learn.

"Apfel deserves another great ruler."

"Thank you?" Snow says. She's surprised by how much it cheers her up to hear this. Amalia knew her mother; can she see something of Snow's mother in her?

But then Amalia prowls toward her, and Snow backs away.

Amalia comes forward.

Snow goes back.

"I think Lucille's up to something," Snow murmurs, pushing down the prickle of unease in her throat. "I'm worried . . . I'm worried she wants the throne."

Amalia continues forward.

Snow goes back. Her elbow bumps against the edge of the mirror.

"It will not only be you thanking me," Amalia growls, "when Apfel gets its rightful queen."

"Just a week away," Snow says cheerfully, although she feels far less cheerful than she sounds. Amalia's expression isn't exactly . . . kind. Like maybe Snow didn't read this situation correctly. "Lucille . . ."

"It will be a shame you never get to see her take the throne," Amalia says, with a smile so awful it makes Snow tremble.

"Wait. What?"

Amalia shoves her, and Snow glares, because what good is it going to do shoving her into a mirror? Except—

There's no glass against her back.

There's no floor beneath her feet.

And Snow is tumbling . . .

tumbling . . .

tumbling . . .

. . . into nothing.

4

Rose

THIS IS THE STORY OF ROSE:

One day, nearly thirteen years ago, Edel wandered through the Dreamwood near Apfel, collecting foxglove for a Wish, when she happened upon a small basket underneath a rosebush. And inside the basket, a baby. There was no note, no proof of where she might have come from, and so Edel took her in as her own.

That's the story Rose has been told her entire life. A girl born from nothing, like a flower blooming from thin air.

Plenty of children were abandoned in the woods then. Famine had descended upon small hamlets in the eastern Dreamwood, and mothers would give up their babies in the hope that someone wealthier might find them and spare them a horrible fate—Edel hadn't said what exactly happened in starving towns, and Rose didn't really want to ask.

There was also a period where fairies dealt curses like candy, and parents would hide their children in the woods so a curse or a fairy wouldn't find them.

Except a fairy found Rose. And so, apparently, did a curse.

Rose sits cross-legged in the storage room once more and depetals a basketful of pink oleander. Oleander means "caution" in the language of flowers—someone sent Edel a Wish to be able to sniff out bad investments. These petals will join several other plants in a mortar and be ground with a pestle into a pulp, whispered to, and brewed into an elixir in a tiny bottle.

Rose wants nothing more than to be alone, and the storage room is the only place she can get some privacy. At least Edel is giving her that, since she won't give her any answers.

Even though Edel *never told her she was cursed.*

Cursed.

Cursed cursed cursed.

Who would do that to her? What did it mean to be cursed? Is she just going to fall asleep one day and stay like that? Do you age in an unwaking sleep? And what about . . . what about going to the bathroom?

"If you don't want to look so sad, maybe you shouldn't have locked yourself in such a dirty pantry."

Rose leaps up, pink petals scattering over the stone floor.

A man with shockingly silver hair and a shockingly blue suit leans against the shelves, beaming at Rose.

"How did you . . . ? Who are you?" Rose splutters. Is *this* the curse? Is this how it starts?

"I was going to pop in on Edel," he says, "but then I saw you sitting here looking quite glum and thought . . . well, that's interesting."

Rose narrows her eyes. "I've never seen you before," she says. Rose has met everyone who's passed through the cottage. Or so she thought. Clearly, there *are* a few things Edel keeps from her.

"Ah. Edel's an old friend. Durchdenwald, at your service." He sweeps into a low bow and pauses. He looks up at her expectantly. "Most people clap afterward."

"Oh. Um, welcome. What do you want?" Rose asks. She's met enough magical folk to know he's a fairy. But Edel hadn't said anything about him coming.

"Oh. Funny little curse business happening over here and over there. Not *all* my doing, of course, but still. Thought I'd, *ahem,* stop by."

She knows why she recognizes his name. He was involved with the curse near Miravale a few months ago, with the beast, the glass slippers, and an enchanted castle. Everyone in the Dreamwood's been talking about it, but not everything they've had to say about *him* was that nice.

"This is about my curse," Rose realizes. He's come to help her. "The sleeping thing."

Durchdenwald frowns. "Why would you be cur—" His eyes widen in shock. "You don't say," he says. "So, Edel's been keeping quite the secret, has she?"

"What do you mean?" Rose presses.

"No. Don't ask me. The Dreamwood Council has clearly forbidden me from getting involved in curse-related business." Durchdenwald holds up his hands and pouts, as if he's never heard anything so tragic.

"Wai—"

Rose thinks she hears rain, and Durchdenwald is gone.

If no one is going to help her, maybe she can be her own fairy godparent. . . .

She scans the plants.

What Wish does Rose even have? That whoever cursed her will come by for tea and explain things?

It turns out that even being cursed, Rose wants what she usually wants: A little bit more power and knowledge than is given to her. To understand. So life doesn't just *happen* to her.

At the very top of the right-hand shelves are the most dangerous plants Edel keeps in the cottage. . . . They might be capable of answering a Wish so big and not yet formed. . . .

Rose shoves a crate near them, clambers on top, stretches up her hands toward the henbane. It's often used in beauty

Wishes to give you wide, doe-like eyes, but maybe it could help her see more, discover more about this curse. . . .

Something hooks itself between Rose's shoulders, yanking her back.

And Rose is falling.

But where there should be the floor to catch her, she's just—

Falling.

5

Snow

S NOW CRASHES INTO THE MUD.

Swallowing a very un-princess-like screech, she squelches up, slipping and sliding in the muck until she can get to her feet.

"Hello?" she calls, spitting out a bit of mud. She tries to wipe her mouth, but her sleeve is faring no better.

This. Is. So. Disgusting.

How *dare* Amalia trick her, after Snow hoped that she was on Snow's side. Clearly, Amalia is still just doing Lucille's dirty work. What is this? Some plot to keep Snow from her Crown Ceremony so that Lucille can take the throne? She won't get rid of Snow that easily.

And . . . and how *dare* Snow be so gullible, so naive?

How is she ever supposed to be a queen if it took Amalia all of five minutes to lure her through a magic mirror?

Snow has no idea where she is. It's a garden of some sort, but certainly not any garden near Apfel. For one, it's not very tidy, flowers and vegetables growing willy-nilly. And it's warmer, with no hint of the fall chill that's tickling Apfel.

"Hello?" Snow calls again. Whenever she moves, her slippers make a slurping sound, mud sloshing around her toes. At this point, it's possible that mud has entered her bloodstream.

Instead of a castle, there's a squat cottage with a thatched roof and a ribbon of smoke rising from the chimney.

And there are an awful lot of trees.

A lot of tall, old-looking pine trees that seem to go up so high they're propping up the turquoise-blue sky and seem to march on so endlessly there's no world beyond them.

"Oh no," Snow whispers. "No. No. No, no, no."

This can't be happening.

She can't possibly be in the Dreamwood, can she?

You don't go into the Dreamwood alone, and you especially don't go beyond its edges. Even though the kingdom of Apfel is plunked straight in its center, Snow's never stepped more than a few feet beyond the city's borders, and only with Prof, her main tutor, to study young unicorns or certain types of ferns.

"Amalia!" Snow screeches.

A plump, short woman with flour all over her apron bustles out of the cottage but falls back when she sees Snow.

"What are you— How are you— You shouldn't— Where's Rose?" The woman's eyes widen, and she surges past Snow, yelling, "Rosie! *Rose!*"

The woman, green with fear, rushes back into the cottage. *"Rosie!"*

Whoever Rose is doesn't seem to be there.

Snow plucks a leaf from a fig tree and tries to scrape off the mud, but whatever's in Dreamwood mud just makes the leaf turn into ten more leaves—all of which cling to her dress.

The woman strides back to glare at Snow, who continues to fail to get the leaves off her dress.

"Did you see her?" the woman demands. "Rose?"

Snow shakes her head. "Is that your cat?"

The woman stares at Snow more closely. Her eyes widen, and she wipes some of the mud off Snow's face with her thumb.

"You," she breathes. "By Grimm. I didn't think I'd be seeing—" Her eyes widen further. "That's why she's gone."

"I think I should be gone, too," Snow suggests. They'll get this all sorted, and soon, so soon, the castle maids will be taking away her dirty garments, pulling her a hot bath, and setting out spiced rolls.

"You look just like her," the woman says, as though Snow hasn't spoken. "I always wondered how you turned out. It could have so easily been you instead. . . ."

Snow frowns. She doesn't have time for whatever

this is. Of course Amalia has managed to hurl her into the Dreamwood with a babbling old woman. Hopefully, she isn't the type of old woman who shoves children into ovens and sucks on their bones for dessert.

"Okay," Snow says. "So how do I get back? Do you have another mirror I can just, I don't know, step through?"

"A mirror?" The woman pauses. "What's this about a mirror?"

Snow hesitates. What if . . . what if the woman is working with Lucille, lurking here to finish Snow off?

The woman stares out at the Dreamwood, frowning. "A magic mirror, of course. She must have gotten her hands on one. Tricky, tricky. If only we had—"

"How do I get back?" Snow asks.

"I can't interfere, Snow," she says, and Snow is more startled that this woman dares to call her by her name than by the fact that she knows who she is. "After what happened with the princess of Miravale, it's too dangerous."

"What happened with her was a wish gone wrong, wasn't it?" Snow says. "I don't care about wishes. I need to get back."

After the Miravale curse, Snow went to visit Prince Amir and his parents, but since the princess wasn't there, it was dull. Amir scribbled letters to some girl named after a bell, and Snow was bored to death as Lucille charmed the royal family.

"Edel," the woman says.

"Excuse you," Snow says.

"I'm Edel." The woman frowns. "If you're going to be

demanding my help, the least we can do is introduce ourselves."

"But you know who I am," Snow says.

The woman huffs. "You're certainly a princess, aren't you?"

Snow's not sure what that means, so she just plants her hands on her hips and frowns. Usually that works.

"No matter. You can't go back to Apfel."

"I can," Snow says. "And I will."

Edel shakes her head. "I promised your mother I would keep you and . . . that I would keep you safe."

"You . . . knew my mother?" Snow asks. Longing sparks in her chest.

"I assume that's why the mirror brought you here." The woman tilts her head. "Magic mirrors tend to have a mind of their own. Now, try not to touch anything that you don't recognize."

"What?"

"In the cottage."

"I'm not going in there," Snow says. Snow has a castle waiting for her. Although if there's a bath . . . The mud is making her skin itch.

The woman stares at her. "Don't be ridiculous," she says, her tone a little sharper. "You're lucky that mirror knew me, or who knows where you would have shown up. You'll wait in my cottage. There will be plenty of food and drink. I'll be back soon. A week, or maybe two, to get it all straightened out."

Snow gapes. A week. Or *two?*

"There's the Crown Ceremony," Snow says weakly. It's in exactly a week, on her birthday. The rules are strict: if a princess does not arrive at her Crown Ceremony, the throne passes to the next eligible ruler. In this case, the queen consort. Lucille. It's happened only once, when Princess Wanda fled to live as a librarian in a small village. But surely if Snow is missing, they'll make an exception. Unless they think she's intentionally gone.

Snow fights down panic. She can't miss the Crown Ceremony. Her entire life has been leading up to this. Sometimes she's not even sure she'll really exist until that crown is laid on her head, accepting her as the next queen of Apfel and bestowing its power upon her.

"Stubborn, too, aren't you?" The woman tuts. "There are dark forces at play, dear. It's not your battle to fight."

"There aren't any battles," Snow argues. "I have to get back."

"You're days away from Apfel," Edel continues. "Weeks, if you try and bypass the deepest of the Dreamwood."

What she's saying is, you can leave by yourself, but you won't get back.

Snow rolls her eyes. "Fine."

She has no choice. She can't be in the Dreamwood by herself. But she has a plan: as soon as Edel leaves, Snow will write to the dwarfs for help.

"Oh, one moment!" Edel calls as Snow trudges to the cottage.

"What?"

"We have to do something about your hair."

"Ex*cuse* me?"

Her hair is long, halfway to her waist. It's a point of pride, brushed a hundred times every morning and every night, washed with egg whites to make it shine, and drenched with rosewater to make it smell sweet.

"It's far too recognizable."

"No!"

"It's for your own good, Snow White."

Snow glares at her. "It's hair," she shoots back. "Everybody has it."

Her hair, her father says, looks just like her mother's. Snow has so few things of hers. She's not parting with it.

But . . . Lucille went through the trouble of finding a magic mirror to push Snow through. A little disguise won't hurt. Although this is another reason to be furious with Lucille.

"Fine," Snow says gruffly, waiting for Edel to run inside and grab a pair of scissors.

Instead, the woman twists her hands in the air.

Snow gasps when she feels a breeze against the back of her neck.

"Much better," Edel says.

Snow swallows a moan.

Her beautiful, beautiful hair, now just glossy black strands scattered over the ground. Her hair is chopped straight below her ears, feeling thick and puffy.

"How?"

Edel plucks a star-shaped white flower off a bush. It's myrtle. Snow recognizes it only because it was her mother's favorite. She has a plant in her room.

"Myrtle. It means 'love.' But if you do this"—Edel turns it upside down and tucks it into Snow's bodice— "then people won't recognize you. It becomes the opposite of love. Indifference." The woman pats Snow's cheek. "But don't get too bold. If they know you quite well, the magic won't be strong enough to protect you."

Snow stares, baffled. "How do you know that? And how did you . . . my hair?"

Edel winks. "Fairies tend to know a thing or two."

She's a *fairy*?

"But . . . ," Snow begins. Surely, she can manage a bit more help than a *flower and a haircut*.

"Don't open the door for anyone, Snow White."

Edel vanishes.

Fiddling with her chopped hair, Snow stomps her way into the cottage, which is cozier than she expected and smells like bread. There are twigs, cut flowers, pots, and vials everywhere. Are they filled with magic? Snow could try to find out . . . but the last thing you do is mess around with magic you don't understand. She could turn to stone or transform into a snail.

Snow can't believe there's all this fuss because that woman's cat is missing.

She doesn't intend to wait here long enough to find

out if the cat's okay. She has to get to the Crown Ceremony. Her mother was queen, and her grandmother. Snow has always been *going to be queen.* Her mother gave up her life to have a daughter, a daughter who would be a good, strong ruler for the kingdom, so that's what Snow has to be. And the Crown Ceremony . . .

When the crown first graces a worthy queen's head, she's visited by the ghosts of the queens who came before her.

For the first and only time in her life, Snow will get to speak to her mother. And she won't let Lucille take that away from her.

Snow scrubs herself off as best she can in the deep kitchen sink, attacking the dried mud with a dishcloth.

She'll contact the dwarfs. Bootes and the rest of them.

But . . . but what if Lucille is intercepting the pigeons? What if Snow really is in danger? Why does everything have to be so *complicated*?

Snow stifles a scream and stamps her feet on the wooden floor. For once she doesn't have to worry if that's princess-like behavior, because there's no one around to—

"Oy, Edel?" A boy's voice seeps into the cottage.

Snow drops to the ground, scrambling to hide. The curtains are pulled back from the windows, and anyone could see her.

"Edel?" the boy calls again.

Snow's heart is beating so fast she's positive its furious pounding is visible through the fabric of her dress.

"EDEL!" he tries again. "You didn't forget about us, did ya?"

At the castle, you would never yell. It's unseemly to behave that way. And it makes Snow prickle with curiosity.

She crawls over to the window, lifting her eyes above the sill.

There's a boy probably around her age with shoulder-length brown hair and a patched leather coat. He rocks back and forth on his heels as he scans the cottage.

"Where is she?" the boy wonders aloud.

Snow's fingers skim over the myrtle in her bodice. Her mother's myrtle blooms every year on Snow's birthday.

Snow's never missed it. And she's not going to miss its blooms now.

Snow flings the door open.

"Edel left," she says.

In all the stories that Snow has heard about the other queens, none of them spent time hiding away.

She's not going to be the first. Especially because that would be really, really embarrassing when people talk about her.

"Left?" The boy spins on his heel, staring at Snow with surprise. Up closer, he's a lot scruffier. And a little handsome. There's a bruise on his wrist and dirt smeared over his cheekbones. One of his eyebrows is bone white. "What'd she do that for? When's she coming back?"

"I don't know," Snow says. She tilts her chin up so it

feels like she's looking down at him. For some reason, this dirty boy makes her stomach twist into knots.

"Who are you?" the boy asks. "Where's Rose?"

Everyone's so concerned. This must be one amazing cat.

"I'm . . ." She only hesitates for a second. "Myrtle."

"Great." He eyes her like he thinks she might be a bit slow on the uptake. "That's not what I asked."

"They're both gone," Snow snaps, because you can't talk down to a princess. "Can you tell me where I can get a carriage?"

The boy whistles, amused. "Only if you can tell me where I can get a flying pig. If you see Edel, let her know the Huntsmen came by. Needed her help with this new Hunt . . ." He shrugs, momentarily distracted by a snail inching over a large rock. "And wanted her lemon loaf."

The Huntsmen?

They're known across Reverie; they can find whatever needs tracking down, from oversized rats nibbling on people's gooseberry plants to magical teapots that've sprouted legs and run away. That's not a bad group to run into.

The boy ambles back into the woods.

Snow gnaws on her bottom lip. Edel was expecting these Huntsmen.

Maybe there's . . .

Snow tears back into the house and forages among the vials and pots on the table for something, anything, she could give them in exchange for help.

It's even better than she could hope. There's a pewter pot with a string tied around it and a note in beautiful, looping cursive: *The Huntsmen*.

Snow seizes the pot and clutches it awkwardly to her chest—it's about the size of a very plump rabbit—and hurtles back through the garden and into the woods in the direction the boy went.

It's only when she stops for breath and glances around her that she realizes going into the woods might not have been a great idea.

She doesn't recognize anything. Everything is forest. Large trees. Little animals scurry among bright green ferns, and the only other sound is the trickling of a nearby stream.

Snow spins around, and nothing changes. She's not exactly sure which way she came. She thought she was following a path, but it's like the forest sucked the path into itself.

Her arms clamp around the pot, and she really wishes there were a genie inside rather than whatever's being given to the Huntsmen.

But before Snow can take another step, a net soars over her, sweeping her into the air.

6

Rose

I'LL TAKE A— *BY GRIMM!*"

"What's going— *Quickly! Out of the way.*"

Footsteps pound. A door slams.

Rose blinks her eyes open blearily.

She stares in confusion at the room around her, but as she starts to push herself upward, her hand lands in a cake.

"*What?*" Rose whispers.

She scrambles upright, trying to wipe frosting off on her dress, but—this doesn't make any sense.

Moments ago, she was in the storage room. She was reaching for henbane, and there was that fairy, Durchdenwald. . . .

Now she's standing, covered in cake, in what must be a bakery. It's narrow, hardly any wider than the shelves used to store the loaves of crusty bread and the fruit-filled pastries. On a wooden sign on the wall, someone painstakingly carved THE FAVORITE BAKERY OF THE QUEENE AND KING. And bright golden sunlight splashes over the strangest bit of all:

A baker, next to Rose.

A shop assistant.

A mousing cat.

A customer.

And all of them . . . asleep.

The baker is propped against a loaf of half-formed dough, his face sinking into it. The shop assistant is sprawled on the floor with two Danish pastries tight in her grasp. The cat looks like it collapsed mid-run, its legs splayed out. The customer snores over one of the display cases.

It's so strange that it takes Rose a moment to realize what she's seeing.

"Hello?" she whispers. Then, louder, because she *wants* to wake them: "Hello!"

No one stirs, not even the cat.

"Hello?" she cries again, but she knows it's not going to work. Magic hangs around this bakery, but not the cozy kind of magic she associates with Edel. This is cold and metallic, utterly still, like time itself has stopped ticking.

Her pulse accelerates. Is sleep coming for her?

Is this the end?

Rose pinches the inside of her elbow, her upper arm,

her cheek. It all hurts. She's awake, at least for right now, but the terror of it feels like it's searing her from the inside out.

"This way, this way!" a voice echoes through the open window. "The sleeping curse has hit the bakery!"

She should get out of here. Maybe curses hang around in the air like illnesses. She starts to scramble toward the door as a man in a strange cream-colored suit bursts inside. He's followed by two guards clunking in gleaming armor.

"What—" the man splutters at Rose.

This does look suspicious. Hopefully, they don't think she's stealing.

"I don't—" is all Rose can mumble, because she doesn't know what's going on, she doesn't know where she is, and she doesn't know *why* she's here.

"You said the sleeping curse hit," the guard with a flower-shaped birthmark on his cheek accuses. "There's a girl quite awake right there."

"But she was . . . I *just* saw her lying there. . . ." The man points weakly at the spot where Rose awoke. "I know it's her. Got that little bag." Rose pats her belt bag; she always has it around her hips to store and collect ingredients.

Fear streaks over his face. "She's the *Night Witch*!" the man declares.

The other guard, who has a pointy little goatee, squeaks.

So does Rose, out of sheer surprise. Her, the Night Witch? Who is supposed to be hundreds of years old and horribly terrible? Rose is covered in cake.

"No one can wake up from the sleeping curse," the flower-marked guard mutters. He lowers the face shield of his helmet, like this will protect him from whatever sorcery Rose might possess.

"Night Witch, I tell you!" the man calls.

The two guards exchange concerned looks.

"She doesn't look much like the Night Witch, Titch," one mutters. "I think."

"That's exactly what the Night Witch would want you to think, wouldn't she, Middles?" The other squints at Rose through his helmet.

"*She* ought to know about this," Titch groans.

"I'm not the Night Witch," Rose clarifies.

Behind the guards, the man who found Rose backs away, bumping against the bakery's doorframe before sprinting down the street.

Each guard grabs one of Rose's arms and steers her outside. She winces. Her cotton dress is light, designed for the permanent balmy springtime around the woodcutter's cottage, not the cold lancing toward them now.

Rose's mouth drops open. The streets are winding and narrow, the buildings tall and different colors. They're in a *city*. How far has she come? The nearest town is days away from the cottage, if you have a horse.

Titch frowns. "Were you or were you not sleeping in this bakery?"

"I was," Rose admits. Wasn't she? She's not exactly sure. "But . . ."

"And did you or did you not *awaken* in this bakery?"

Rose stares at him. "I . . . did," she says. "But—"

"Night Witch," Middles breathes.

"I'm not the Night Witch!" Rose exclaims, trying to remain calm, even while panic starts to creep up.

"That's what the Night Witch would say!" Titch cries. "By the order of the, uh . . . what's it called?"

The other guard whispers into his ear. Titch clears his throat.

"By the order of the Anti-Curse Regulation Task Force, you're under arrest."

7

Snow

NOW, NOW. WHAT DO WE HAVE HERE?"

What they have is Snow squirming, her eyes screwed tight, within a net that smells slightly soiled. It swings with even the smallest motion, and her stomach lurches. She hates heights. Hates hates hates.

"A little peasant girl, is it?" asks a man with a voice thin as watered-down milk. "Ah, poor thing."

Peasant girl?

Despite how much Snow wants to convince herself that she's on solid ground, she still manages to glare down at them.

A troop of people in ragged leather glare up at her.

"A harmless little thing," a woman with a shaved head declares. "And she's scared! Let her down, Ivan."

"I am *not* scared!" Snow declares, because there is no way she's going to let these people say they caught the princess of Apfel and she was afraid of heights.

"'A harmless little thing' is exactly what a *not*-harmless *not*-little thing would want you to think!" says a large man who has silver hair and a silver beard and looks like a polar bear. His accent sounds like it's from the North, the vowels hitting hard and long. Snow's always liked that accent.

She likes it a little less right now.

"The only thing you need to think about is getting me down," Snow commands.

"Hey." The boy with the one white eyebrow trots over. She twists in the ropes, grimacing as they chafe against her skin. This net had better not leave a scar. "I know her, Ivan."

"Let. Me. Go," she directs in her most queenly voice, even though she feels frightened and not queenly at all.

"You know her?" the tall man asks.

"You don't know anyone, Dimitri," the woman with the shaved head says.

"Sure I do," the boy says, puffing out his chest. "Met her at Edel's."

"Edel's?" The man looks interested. "Friend of Rosie's, then, are you?"

What is it with Dreamwood people and this cat?

"You forgot this!" Snow squirms around so the pot is visible. "Thought you might need it."

"Well, why didn't you start with that!" The man claps his hands. Apparently, Snow is no longer deemed a threat. "Let her down, fellas."

Snow doesn't have a moment to brace herself before the net releases and she plummets to the ground, landing in a pile of scratchy rope.

The boy hurries over to her, looking bemused. "Are you okay?" he whispers, offering her a hand. Dimitri, the woman called him.

She pushes herself up. Being suspended from a net is humiliating enough. Needing a boy's help is even worse.

"I would be better if I hadn't been treated like a wild rabbit before stew day," she whispers back, an old saying of her father's. He'd picked up slang from throughout Reverie; Snow always liked the way the phrases felt to say, as though her life has been full of more adventures.

"If you had given me the pot when I came by, nets wouldn't have been required." He grins, like they're sharing a joke. It catches Snow off guard.

"Where's the fun in that?" Snow mutters. She expects Dimitri to be mad, but instead his grin broadens.

"And what strange little creature did Edel send into our midst?" The polar bear–like man peers inquisitively at Snow. His face is craggy, his nose uneven, with a chunk missing from the tip.

But it's not a man.

None of them are men or women.

Unlike Edel, they're clearly not human. Their skin has a silver tint to it, and the tips of their ears are slightly pointed. Fairies. That explains why they're so good at finding things.

"Myrtle," Dimitri, who looks like an ordinary boy, says, "meet the Huntsmen."

"It's an old name," the fairy with the shaved head mutters. "There are females now, too."

Snow's relieved. She thought that her return home would involve fewer nets, but she didn't think she'd get lucky enough to find the Huntsmen. Surely, they can make short work of any distance. And maybe force Lucille to back down.

"So." Ivan looks surprised that he's not yet in possession of the pot. Snow hugs it tighter. "Kind of you to bring it out here. Do you . . . Is it payment you want?"

At first Snow's annoyed. Does she look like a messenger? But then she remembers that's a good thing. She's not *supposed* to look like a princess.

"I need help getting to Apfel," she says. "Something just . . . There's been some . . . It's complicated. But I need to get there."

"Apfel?" Dimitri asks.

"We're not taking another, Ivan," the Huntsman with the shaved head warns the polar bear fairy. She narrows her eyes like Snow is a small bug on an apple she's eating: a minor annoyance. But she doesn't scare Snow. Snow, after all, has a stepmother who got her shoved through a magic mirror.

"I really need to get back," Snow says. "Please. I won't be a bother."

She can't wait to see Lucille's face when the gates of Apfel fling open and there stands Snow, triumphant, a squadron of some of Reverie's most renowned fairies behind her.

"Perhaps we can spare . . ." Ivan starts to relent before the fairy with the shaved head can protest. He adds hurriedly, "But times aren't what they used to be. Passage can't be granted free. What can you do? Clean?"

"Um . . ."

"Sew?"

"Um."

"Cook?"

"Um."

Ivan's woolly eyebrows dagger together. "I'm supposed to believe that a girl who can't do much earned Edel's respect?"

"I *can* do things," Snow protests.

For instance, she can curtsy. Kind of waltz. She knows which fork to use for which dish of a twelve-course meal. She can whistle a bawdy dwarven mining tune.

Worry pools in her stomach. What if she can't do much? What if this stranger can look at her and see the truth?

"We're wasting time, Ivan," the fairy with the shaved head says.

"I can . . . sing to birds," Snow blurts, panicked at the possibility of being left behind. The Huntsmen eye her. She knows that it sounds like a weird, useless lie.

All Apfel princesses are born with a thin stream of magic in their blood, an inheritance from Nora, the First Queen. Some are brilliant warriors. Some move rocks with their mind. Some create such beautiful drawings, they can subdue enemies. Snow's mother could master any song on any instrument, a skill that made her popular even among the nastiest of the orcs and the goblins. And Snow can get birds to zoom in different directions, which has never felt that *useful*.

Finally, it seems like it's coming in handy.

Ivan folds his arms.

"Show us."

This is so embarrassing. Snow hates performing, in case she messes up, but she really needs the Huntsmen's help to get to Apfel. Snow clears her throat and tries to whistle, but her mouth is too dry. All she manages to do is croak.

The Huntsmen stare at her. The fairy with the shaved head coughs. Dimitri gives an encouraging smile.

Snow takes a deep breath, swallows, and then whistles. Out comes a jaunty tune, a little anxious and uncontrolled, but at least a melody. Four falcons swoop down from the sky, swirling together above Snow in a great circle. She can sense their restlessness, their dreams for endless sky.

All the Huntsmen look impressed, staring either at her or at the birds.

Snow whistles a little while longer, wishing hawks were strong enough to pick her up and take her home. When she stops the song, the birds flutter away.

"You see that, Olive?" Ivan exclaims to the fairy with the shaved head. "That's not too shabby."

"Why do you want to get back so badly?" Olive asks, suspicious. "It's safer being away. With everything that's going on."

Safer away? But—

"*What's* going on?" Snow asks.

Lucille's hint. Bootes's warning. Now this.

"The curse," Olive says. She tilts her head. "I thought word had spread faster."

Snow stares, sure she's misheard. A curse? In Apfel? Impossible. She was *just there*. She's the *princess*. Surely, she would know if there's a curse.

"Curse," Snow repeats.

"Marie's gone now," Dimitri cuts in. "Myrtle could have her bed. And it was helpful having another human around."

"There you have it." Ivan claps his hands. "A free bed, and you never know when birdsong will come in handy out here. Let's get on with it, then. Wasted too much time already."

"Really?" Snow asks, temporarily forgetting what Olive said. "You'll take me?"

It worked. She'll get back for her Crown Ceremony. And the look on Lucille's face will be worth all the mud.

"Next thing you know, we'll let nobles rent out the train to get to the Ten Falls!" Olive throws up her hands, then grows serious. "Myrtle. You have to understand that this isn't an easy journey."

Ivan nods. "We're hunting someone very dangerous. Someone very tricky, very dastardly, very wicked. The person they believe started the curse on Apfel."

"Okay," Snow says. She just needs to get to Apfel. That will take about two minutes with fairy magic, probably. A rumor about a nonexistent curse isn't going to scare her away.

"And we can't promise that you won't be in harm's way," Olive says.

"Who are you hunting?" Snow asks.

This could end up sounding good in the stories: Snow, the brave figurehead during one of history's most revered Hunts.

"We're hunting," Olive says, like she's almost savoring the words, "the princess of Apfel. Snow White."

8

Rose

ROSE STARES AT THE GUARDS.

"I'm *twelve*," she clarifies.

"A cunning disguise," Middles whispers.

At this point, Rose wouldn't mind being the Night Witch. A little magic wouldn't hurt right now.

But if other members of the Anti-Curse Regulation Task Force are as thickheaded as these guards and think her a centuries-old villain because she *woke up*, how is she supposed to explain that she was whisked from a storage room in the Dreamwood to a bakery in a city she's never visited?

"Don't try any of your magic on us," Titch grunts.

"I'll do my best," Rose says.

Surely, if she had magic, she would have *poof*ed away

from them by now. And surely, if a sleeping curse is falling upon the city, there's a much greater danger than a girl covered in cake.

The guards lead her into a larger avenue, and Rose gasps. People bundled in furs wander around. A few vendors swirl wooden paddles through steaming vats of cider. Rising high above the city stands a white-and-blue castle.

A castle she recognizes from books, pamphlets, stories.

It's Apfel. Rose has fantasized about it so much that it almost doesn't feel real. Admittedly, this wasn't how she imagined arriving. But the RAA is here.

Her . . . her family could be here.

The guards take her to a small, thin carriage, pulled by a bored-looking purple mule with thick hooves. They bind her hands behind her with rope.

"Get on it, then," Titch orders.

"I didn't do anything wrong," Rose says.

But . . . what other choice does she have? She's not sure how to get back to Edel, and a castle sounds like the best place to get help. Surely someone will have more common sense than these guards. Rose climbs into the carriage, sitting atop a bale of hay.

"She's being too polite," Middles whispers.

"Must be a trick. Here." Titch pulls out a dirty rag and gestures for the other to tie it around Rose's eyes. "They can't cast magic if they can't see."

Rose is pretty positive this isn't true, but she's not going to waste time arguing. The image of the people cut down by sleep in the middle of baking, selling, ordering bread—it makes her shiver.

She tenses as Middles wraps the blindfold around her eyes. Then she listens as the guards get into the front of the carriage.

Rose sways and grips the hay in her fists as the carriage lurches over the cobblestones, around bends, and up the hill. Her fingers grow cold, even as she digs them deeper into the stalks.

People chatter and whistle and haggle. Donkeys clop, coins clink, accordions bellow. A bell tower clangs, dogs woof, newsies hawk papers . . . and Rose wonders how much of the chattering has to do with people seeing a blindfolded girl in the back of a royal guard carriage.

She's imagined, countless times, arriving in Apfel, perhaps with a smart leather satchel, a notebook, phoenix-feather quills, and an acceptance letter from the RAA saying she was the top applicant by a mile. It's too bad you can't make dreams true just by wanting them enough.

Finally, the carriage stops. The blindfold is ripped off, but the guards keep her hands tied.

Rose hops down eagerly. Her legs are cramping, and the cold has seeped into her bones. What she would give for a dry dress and a crackling fire. Or just home.

They stand in the center of a resplendent castle court-yard. It's bustling with townspeople who crane over the low walls surrounding the courtyard to stare at the Dream-wood ablaze in autumn colors, a merchant passing burlap sacks to servants, a few nobles arguing with an important-looking man who is wearing a lemon-colored coat and carrying a thick stack of papers. The castle rises above them: its white spires, its parapets, its stained-glass windows.

At first, no one pays any attention to them.

Except for . . .

A boy whose shoulders are hunched slightly and who looks uncomfortable with how tall he is. He stares at them, open-mouthed.

The guards must feel the intensity of his gaze, because Middles snaps his fingers. "You, there! Boy! Go and get the damafrau!"

The boy's blue eyes widen. Rose finds it hard to stop looking at him: he has a narrow face and white-blond hair, and his clothes are very clean and sharp. The only other human boy she's seen up close is Dimitri, and this one seems like a different specimen.

"Are you deaf?" Titch demands.

"Oh-ho." A large nobleman dressed in peach-colored silks chuckles at them. "Don't you know who that is? That's Sir York Petrifer."

But the boy has already scurried away. The guards seem troubled.

"How were we supposed to know? All kids look the same, don't they?" Titch mutters.

"Is he one of them important nobles?" Middles mutters back.

They, Rose thinks, aren't very good at their jobs. Some of the other nobles and merchants are turning toward them, and it makes her heart race a little bit faster. She just wants to get home.

The tall boy scurries back, panting a little and clutching his side.

"She's in the throne room," he says.

"We thank you with great appreciation, honorable Sir York," Middles says, bowing deeply, and the boy's face scrunches, confused.

He tags along as the guards haul Rose forward.

"What'd *you* do?" the boy asks. Rose ignores him because she doesn't know how to explain it. At all.

Their grip is rough as Rose stumbles to keep up. In the castle, it smells like mint and eucalyptus, and they stride through ornate halls, across gleaming wooden floors, underneath diamond flowers dangling from the ceiling, past golden weapons mounted on the walls.

This is . . . incredible. Rose has a vibrant imagination, but not even her imagination could conceive of *this*.

Finally, they pause outside a set of double doors at least twice Rose's height.

"You shouldn't be here," the boy whispers, then scampers away down a corridor.

Rose stares after him, stunned, before the guards drag her inside and all other thoughts dissolve.

The walls sweep up high, the wood intricately carved

with what must be moments in Apfel's history: queens charging into battle, queens standing before bountiful harvests, queens negotiating with basilisks.

Rose could spend all afternoon staring at them, but they're not even the most impressive feature. Light drifts through the glass half-dome ceiling, over two gnarled, bare apple trees in the center of the room and a throne that looks like it's made out of thousands of leaves. Behind it, on a pedestal, is the Apfel crown, elegant and small, with swooping silver designs and two pearls in the center, one white and one black. Even from here, Rose can feel the vibrations of its magic.

"*What* is *that?*" a woman asks. She wears a stiff gray dress and her nose twitches like she's smelling something awful.

Rose hadn't even realized the woman was standing there. The guards recoil as soon as she speaks.

Rose doesn't blame them. The woman looks like someone who would enjoy getting you into trouble. Someone who would rather eat a bowl of cold sardines than ice cream.

"We think it's a child," Titch says.

"How very astute of you," the woman says. "It's a wonder we don't pay you to think more."

The guards exchange glances. Middles clears his throat.

"The sleeping curse struck some of the merchants in the Old Quarter," he says. "And we found *her* awake. We think she might be"—his voice lowers—"the Night Witch."

"I can absolutely assure you this is not the Night Witch," the woman scoffs.

She turns her attention to Rose, and the force of her gaze makes Rose's skin crawl, but there's something so familiar—

"You're Lady Amalia!" Rose declares.

The woman stares at her. "Yes," she says stiffly. "So I am."

"Normally, people don't sound so enthusiastic about that," Middles whispers into Rose's ear.

Rose blushes. "I've always wanted to meet the Apfel damafrau," she confesses. No one else in the Wood cares so much about royalty, but she gobbles up as much news as she can, and she's heard plenty about Lady Amalia. The queen's right hand. It's the closest Rose has ever come to a queen, and she can't wait to tell Edel.

Amalia looks caught off guard by Rose's enthusiasm, but pleased.

A door behind the throne opens, and out glides one of the most beautiful women Rose has ever seen. Her cheekbones are high, her eyes golden, and her pale blond hair drapes over one shoulder. A dragon tattoo curls around the other.

"I heard voices," the woman says. "I thought we were meeting with the alchemists."

The two guards fall to their knees.

Amalia drops into a low curtsy, which is impressive given how stiff her dress looks.

"Bow," she hisses to Rose. "You're in front of the queen."

Rose can't believe it.

That's . . . That's . . .

"There isn't a queen of Apfel," Rose says, in case this is a trap. But she drops into a curtsy. "Queen Elora died a few days after giving birth to Snow White."

Amalia gasps. One of the guards looks like Rose has just made herself the unluckiest person in the world.

"There is a queen consort," Amalia hisses. *"And you are looking at her."*

So. The only trap is the one Rose set for herself, it seems.

But more than Rose's dismay at what she said is her absolute awe at being so close to Lucille. She curtsies again. Maybe if she's lucky, she'll get to see Princess Snow White, too.

Queen Consort Lucille laughs. "I am the closest thing Apfel's kingdom has to a queen. Until the Crown Ceremony, at least."

Rose has to stop herself from staring. News of Lucille's marriage to the king spread deep into the Dreamwood, and the queen consort is everything Rose wants to be: a woman from nowhere with origins murky even to the Dreamwood folk, who gained a family and a place in the world.

"Why is there a girl tied up with rope?" Lucille asks, studying Rose.

Lady Amalia stiffens.

"They say she's awoken from the sleeping curse," she says.

Lucille's body goes rigid, and her gaze burns. She turns her full attention on Rose.

"This is true?" she asks.

Rose feels transfixed. "Yes," she says. "I just . . . I don't think I have the sleeping curse."

Well. That's not true. But it's a bit complicated to get into, especially when she's still trying to make sense of everything.

"We found her in the bakery," Titch pipes up.

"The bakery?" Lucille asks. "The curse has hit again?"

Amalia grimaces. "I wouldn't be surprised at hearing of more before the day is out."

Lucille turns on Rose, and Rose shrinks back. An actual queen is looking at her. "Something terrible is beginning within the Apfelian kingdom. The city is facing the worst of it. This morning, one report of the curse, and then another. Already our best alchemists and healers have been at work, but nothing can wake the sleepers. And yet here you stand."

"She might be the Night Witch," Titch supplies.

"We placed her under arrest," Middles adds helpfully.

Lucille stares at them, frowning. "You should have taken her to the healers," she reprimands. "Is there a curse going around that gets rid of common sense?"

The two guards look like they're not sure what to do next.

Rose is stunned. An actual almost-queen is paying attention to her.

"Remove those ropes. Take her to the healers," Lucille commands. She turns to Rose. "My sincere apologies at how you've been treated. I'll arrange with our lord of hospitality to ensure that you and your family are compensated for this experience."

Middles scrambles forward to unknot the ropes around Rose's wrists. She shakes out her hands. "Could she have anything to do with the missing princess?" Titch blurts.

Rose tries not to look shocked. Snow White is missing?

Lucille turns toward him slowly, frostily. "Don't be ridiculous," she says. "Amalia. The alchemists?"

"I'll bring them. Guards, take her away," Amalia commands.

The guards grab Rose's arms once again.

Rose doesn't have a choice.

She doesn't know what type of magic dropped her in Apfel. But there must be a reason.

The people here are facing the same curse that could be coming for Rose. What is she supposed to do—sit around, twiddle her thumbs, and wait to see whether the curse creeps over her?

Rose calls out: "I came to be one of the alchemists."

Lucille turns toward Rose slowly, the queen-consort's head tilting. There's something about her that reminds Rose of a house built over a fire, the wood warping slightly from the flames within. Rose's heart pounds in her chest. What happens when you lie to a queen?

And she hates lying. It makes her itchy.

"You're a child," Lucille points out.

"You need help," Rose says. "I'm good. I promise. I can make a Dreamweaver's Draught. And I'm . . . starting at the RAA next month."

Mostly true. She can make the draught, with a little guidance. And she *could* be starting at the RAA.

Amalia's eyes narrow. "Oh, marvelous. A student will save us all."

Lucille looks fascinated. "A Dreamweaver's Draught," she says. "That's an odd potion. Quite complicated."

"So the girl's read a few old books!" Amalia exclaims. "Really, my lady."

Lucille's eyebrows arch. "Sometimes the smartest among us can be the young. Letting the girl have a go won't crumble a kingdom, Amalia. At worst, it will be a good lesson for her in humility."

"Come," Lucille says to Rose.

"Come?" Rose repeats.

"I think it would be best if we didn't mention your little curse adventure to anyone." Lucille smiles, but there are layers to that smile, and not all of them seem nice. "Now. Let's see what you can do."

This time, no guards grab her. It is only Amalia's metal gaze that prods Rose forward, only the sense that you can't say no to a queen, especially once you've lied to her.

Lucille sails toward the doors and down a set of stone

steps. The air chills. Rose hugs her arms around her chest and follows.

They reach a cavernous room lit by salt lamps. It has an ancient feel, the ceiling high overhead ribbed with arches. There are three pools: one large, flanked by two smaller. The water's surface reflects everything back, so it's like Rose is standing above another chamber.

A platform floats in the center of the largest pool. Twelve men, half looking confident and the others worried, are seated at tables with a few tools, some vials, and a pile of flowers. Some mutter, and some fiddle with the plants, dropping their hands whenever one of the guards glares at them.

At the queen consort's approach, they all freeze, staring straight ahead as though they're afraid to look at her.

"We've brought in the city's best alchemists," Lucille says softly to Rose. "They have participated in two challenges so far. The best will work with me to find a cure for the sleeping curse. This is their third, and final, challenge. You may join them."

A few of the men twitch as a slim bridge rises out of the water, connecting the platform to the rest of the chamber.

"This is ridiculous," Amalia hisses. "This is private information. A common girl can't be—"

Lucille dismisses Amalia's words. "There aren't any secrets now. Everyone knows there's a curse, and everyone knows there must be a cure. Take a seat, child."

Rose hesitates. She's never brewed a potion in front of

a stranger before, let alone a queen consort, her damafrau, and twelve professional alchemists.

And thirteen is a bit of an unlucky number. Concern prickles at the back of Rose's mind.

But Rose's feet don't seem to hear her brain's worry, because they carry her over the bridge. A guard hustles over a huffy-looking alchemist, with a beard nearly down to his waist, so he can share a table with a stick-thin man with a mean-set mouth. Rose sits in his former seat, her hands pressed between her legs to keep them from shaking. Can you be re-arrested for impersonating an RAA student?

Lucille crosses her arms behind her. The men fall silent.

"A Breath of Fire will suffice, I would think," Lucille declares. The alchemists exchange surprised glances, a few swearing under their breath. "You have one hour."

Rose expects her to depart, but Lucille stays, her golden eyes seeing everything.

No one moves. Rose digs her nails into her palms. In her fantasies of being in Apfel, she's never nervous. A Breath of Fire is an unexpected potion. They made one once for a blacksmith who sought a more powerful forge and signed several contracts promising to use it responsibly. And that took three months to prepare properly.

"The hour has started," Lucille says.

Like a spell has been broken, the alchemists measure, grind with mortars and pestles, pluck off petals, drip in bits of tinctures, and resume muttering at a more intense level than before.

Rose can't believe that she asked to do this. There's a curse coming closer and closer to her. She should be with Edel, not strangers. Edel can make Wishes to fix anything.

But she's here now. And Edel always says that you have to face your fears.

Rose's hands shake so badly that the first time she picks up a stem of hyssop, it falls right back onto the table.

One of the alchemists, a young man with long, greasy brown hair, snorts with laughter.

That's enough to fill Rose with resolve. Especially because the greasy-haired alchemist has added chamomile root, a common mistake, and too innocent an ingredient for something like this. A good potion requires an element of danger.

Rose tears up a few fern fronds for secrecy and crushes them in the mortar and pestle with the hyssop. As she works, she feels calm and confident.

She adds dried poisonous fly amanita and chokevine, combining the crushed mixture in a small vial with water. She leans over it and whispers, "Not being wanted," which is a fear she's never told anyone, but potions require truth.

She's pleased—no one else whispers to their potions.

Ruby steam blooms over her potion's surface like a flower unfurling. Human alchemists are to fairies what a piece of stale toast is to a cake slathered in rich, buttery frosting. Rose might not be a fairy like Edel, but she's learned not just to brew potions but to speak the language of flowers as the fairies do.

"Your time is up," a guard announces.

Rose sits back in her chair. She didn't realize an hour had passed. One hour closer to the curse. She just hopes working on the potion was worth it.

The greasy-haired alchemist peeks at her potion, dark red and coiling in the vial, like a living thing.

"That doesn't seem right," the alchemist observes.

"Then I guess you'll win," Rose replies, because being polite is important. You never know why someone's in a bad mood, Edel says.

"Of course, we can only confirm your skills through a test," Lucille says. "Grab your potions and follow me."

None of the other alchemists seem to be expecting this, either, and the unease is palpable as they stopper their vials, cross the bridge, and follow Lucille back to the throne room.

Rose is last, Amalia coming up behind her, clop-clop-clop.

Lucille stops near the pedestal holding up the Apfel crown. The smile she turns on them reminds Rose of the night sky, like you could get lost in it and never find your way back. "Whoever can destroy the crown will be chosen as the alchemist investigating the curse," she says. "A great honor, one that will surely make your name resonate throughout history. Now, who will go first?"

Amalia hisses.

The alchemists stare at her, all still.

Rose wants to laugh.

Destroy the crown? Rose has no intention of getting arrested again. The crown is more than a symbol. When an Apfel queen puts it on, the magic in her blood intensifies. It's a powerful weapon, and other kingdoms have fought for it, hoping to harness its abilities, but all have failed.

Lucille isn't laughing. She seems annoyed that no one has stepped forward.

"The crown is made of silver from the Smithery," she says. "Enchanted, of course, but a proper Breath of Fire should be able to melt it."

Again, a proper Breath of Fire takes months. And Rose has heard about the crown's enchantments. It can defend itself against attacks, damage, or malicious intent, gravely injuring those who might try to steal or harm it. The Night Witch is unable to pick it up from the pedestal without suffering an even worse fate.

Rose's brow furrows.

"Go on," Lucille urges. "I'm the queen consort. And I give permission."

"We all know I'm going to win anyway." A burly man with long dark hair steps forward, unstoppering his vial.

It's a trick. Rose is pretty sure even a great Breath of Fire can't destroy the crown, and certainly not one brewed in an hour.

An attack on the crown could be disastrous for the person who attempts it. Any alchemist worth their salt should know that.

The alchemist moves to throw the potion at the crown,

and Rose hurls herself at him, smacking the vial from his hand.

The glass explodes on the floor, the potion hissing and writhing harmlessly.

"It's a test," she whispers.

The rest of the room has fallen silent. It's clear Rose has done something horribly, horribly wrong. In front of the queen consort, no less.

The other alchemists do what they do best: they stare at her. How much she wishes she could be staring at a person making a fool of herself, rather than being the fool.

"Out," Lucille purrs, so softly Rose isn't sure if anyone hears, but all the alchemists and guards scurry away and the door slams shut behind them. Rose backs away.

"I'm s-sorry," she stammers.

"Not you." Lucille stalks toward her. "You're not going anywhere."

9

Rose

I'M SORRY." ROSE WINCES. SHE SHOULDN'T have done that. She knows that. But Edel always says to do the right thing, and that man would have been hurt if he'd thrown the potion.

Still. It's probably not good to disobey the queen consort in front of her.

"Most people," Lucille says, "think that alchemy is about cleverness. But compassion is a very overlooked skill."

Rose frowns. Isn't she supposed to be in trouble?

"I want you to help me with a very special project to try and cure this curse." Hands clasped behind her back, Lucille strides over to the apple trees at the center of the throne room.

"You don't even know if my potion worked."

"I was watching you. You knew what you were doing. But more importantly, you thought about the complete picture. It's not just the potion but its consequences. I have many alchemists seeking answers, but I can't trust any of them with such a task as the one I ask of you."

"Shouldn't a fairy help?" Rose asks.

"We've already contacted several. But I want as many minds on this as I can have."

Rose can't really believe what she's hearing. This . . . worked out. She did this, all on her own.

"Don't worry. The Crown doesn't expect work without reward. You'll be given lodgings here. Any food you may want. Access to the RAA facilities as needed. If you succeed in breaking the curse . . . I'll make sure you're well thanked."

"Really?" is all Rose can manage. Her, working with the queen. That's . . . that's the kind of thing you put on an RAA application. That might be better than going to the RAA, period.

"You doubt yourself," Lucille says. "Good. I need that uncertainty to fuel creativity. The days ahead of us will be full of doubt."

With those resources, this is Rose's chance to learn more about this curse, and her curse, and how to break both of them. And to take what she's good at and make something of herself.

"Do you know how Apfel was founded?" Lucille continues when Rose doesn't speak. She gestures toward the trees, bare and blossomless. Where the branches intersect hangs a tiny shiny apple with a sweet, strange smell. Rose can't tell what tree it's from. "Apfel was built by two sisters, back when Reverie was still young. The sisters were witches and created a kingdom where magic could flourish. But they fought over how to rule it."

"I've heard this story." Rose loves it, like she loves most stories with princesses and kingdoms, the epic sagas of royalty.

"Then you know they called the wicked sister the Night Witch because she became corrupted by her desire for power," Lucille continues. "She enacted a curse of unwaking sleep on those who fought against her, before the First Queen defeated her and locked her in the Night Garden in iron shoes that burned her feet whenever she tried to walk. Some worry what's happening now is a sign of her return. I believe they're correct."

"But she's been gone for centuries," Rose says.

Lucille inclines her head. "Indeed. But she escaped the Night Garden following her sister's death, and no one knows where she is. I think she may be back to finally reclaim her throne. I've yet to hear of anyone who can cast a sleeping curse quite like this. And as you heard, my stepdaughter is missing, with wild rumors that she's responsible for what's happening." Lucille's eyes gleam. "I can only imagine the Night Witch's eagerness to get rid of Snow White."

Rose kind of wishes she didn't end up in Apfel at the

same time as the Night Witch. This isn't how it went in her imagination.

"The last time the trees bore an apple was right before the Night Witch gained her greatest amount of power, before she caused the sleeping curse," Lucille says. "And now it blooms again."

She plucks the apple from the tree.

"I believe this may hold some clues to the curse."

She extends it to Rose.

"And you're going to figure out how."

A VERY NERVOUS BUTLER LEADS ROSE ON A TOUR throughout the busy castle—there are the king's quarters, the Hall of Portraits, the Hall of Jewels, the Hall of Scepters, the queen consort's office, the Hall of Swords—and Rose never knew that one place could possess so much magnificence.

The room Rose has been brought to looks like it was built for queens, not guests.

In the woodcutter's cottage, her room is big enough. There's space for her dresser, her bed, and her desk, with the occasional bumped knee.

This room has enough space that Rose could completely stretch out at the foot of the four-poster bed and her fingers wouldn't make contact with the wall. There's an entire separate sitting room *just for her*, with vases filled with lavender, for tranquility. There are so many unfamiliar taps and handles in the bathroom that she's not sure she'll figure out how to get clean. Fluffy robes, folded silk pajamas, beautiful dresses already in her size are waiting in a closet nearly as big as Rose's old bedroom. The windows stretch high and overlook the Dreamwood, evergreens mixed with the reds and golds of fall.

Somewhere out there are home and Edel, although they feel much farther away than a matter of miles. And Snow White. Rose hopes she's okay. The castle is alive with whispers that somehow Snow White is to blame for the curse, which Rose finds hard to believe.

Rose puts the tiny apple on a writing desk and stares out the window. She's filled with a sudden fury at Edel: Edel, who knew about this curse and never once told Rose, never once warned her or thought of a way to prepare her. . . .

Rose throws herself into one of the small chairs in the sitting area and . . . doesn't know what to do next.

This was a terrible idea. Rose has always had Edel's guidance in potion-making. Even in the RAA, they don't make you come up with your own potions until the fourth year. Someone who can *actually* do this should be trying to find a cure—then Rose will have a cure to save herself.

Could she have made everything worse?

And an *apple.* What is she supposed to do with an *apple?*

Rose's stomach rumbles. Maybe what she should do with the apple is eat it.

There's a scraping sound behind her.

She turns.

There's—

The world goes black. Something rough tightens around her wrists.

"If you know what is good for you," a scratchy voice whispers in her ear, "you will not make a sound."

10

Snow

BY THE TIME THE HUNTSMEN ESCORT SNOW to a clearing, she's so deep in wondering just how *bad* this situation is that she doesn't even notice her surroundings.

Because this is *very bad.*

They're hunting her.

And they're fairies. And sooner rather than later, one of them will probably start to wonder why they've encountered Snow-Myrtle right when they're looking for a princess. . . .

But. Wait.

They think she caused a *curse?* Why would they think that?

Because that's what Lucille must be saying. A lie, another trick, to keep Snow from the throne.

Snow thought Lucille was just a vain wife, nursing petty jealousies and dreams of being queen. Not someone who would sic dangerous fairies on a princess.

Maybe she should have listened to Edel and stayed where it was safe.

"Most people are more excited," Dimitri whispers. "Not everyone gets to see the Huntsmen's caravan."

Snow frowns at some kind of lopsided, broken-down train.

It looks like a child got its hands on paint and drew a disjointed snake. Four cars, an engine, and a caboose squat in the center of the Dreamwood. Snow doesn't see any tracks. Each segment is an absurdly bright color—lime green, dandelion yellow, a searing red, a turquoise blue, a pumpkin orange, and lavender for the caboose—though some paint patches have peeled off.

There are tiny, tiny wheels that don't seem like they'd do much good. At the front dangles a large light, like an anglerfish Snow saw at the aquarium once.

"It's . . . ," Snow begins.

"Amazing?" Dimitri exclaims.

That's one word for it. It also happens to be missing tracks.

Other Huntsmen sit around, mending leather goods and playing cards, and Snow tenses as a few look their way, but Dimitri beckons her forward.

"Meet Myrtle!" he announces. "Birds love her."

A bit of an exaggeration. But it got her here.

Dimitri introduces the Huntsmen excitedly, like Snow is supposed to recognize them. There's Mud, a squat man with a seemingly permanent smile, who drives the train. Then white-blond Kaya; Thorne, as massive as a mountain; Garrick, as lean and sharp as a knife; Gregor, with tattoos swirling up and down his body. A few others, who keep to themselves.

Which of them might realize who she is? Should she run away, back to Edel's cottage? Maybe she could contact the dwarfs through birdsong . . . but the dwarfs can't really speak bird.

"How did you get stuck here?" Snow asks.

"Stuck where?" Dimitri asks.

Snow gestures at the train, its lack of tracks.

He grins. "Don't worry about it."

Well, someone should probably be worrying, because the problem with trains is that they aren't any good without tracks.

Dimitri beckons to Snow and points to the first car after the engine.

"C'mon. A tour. This is the common area."

He hops up the stairs to the yellow car, hauling open the door so she can see inside.

Snow winces. It smells like travel, a little like wet socks and sawdust. Dimitri glows with pride.

The car is crammed with sagging leather sofas and bulging bookshelves. On the only available table, someone is building sculptures out of clay: mangled-looking bears, mutant unicorns, and a half-melted dragon. Potted plants dangle from the ceiling. On one wall, someone's mounted a huge map of Reverie. Her heart flips seeing her kingdom's name, the lines marking Apfel's borders and the dot for Apfel the city.

"Is it true?" Snow asks. "About the curse? In Apfel?"

Dimitri looks her up and down. "Course it's true," he says. "I mean, no one's really *surprised*. Everyone's kind of been . . . waiting."

"Waiting?" Snow asks, horrified. For a curse, in her kingdom? Why didn't anyone warn *her*?

"Yeah. No one knows what happened to the Night Witch, right? Folks figured she'd come back and try to get her throne eventually."

Snow can only stare. She's never heard this before. But then again, people don't tell her a lot. She's never invited to meetings with the ministers, like the ideas would be too complicated for her, and she usually only learns about significant Reverie news by overhearing servants. The head librarian even trails her around the library as though Snow must be protected from certain books. The only person who's ever talked about the Night Witch openly in front of her has been Lucille.

"Then why are you hunting the princess?"

"Because she's causing the curse," Dimitri says, like it's obvious. "She's working with the Night Witch."

Snow's stomach falls to her toes. *That's* what people are saying? They think she's in cahoots with her villainous many-times-great-aunt who's been missing for centuries? It's preposterous. But . . . if people *do* start to believe it . . . then they will throw Snow in prison. Or worse. The Night Witch is the kind of haunt that people invoke on All Hallows' Eve or to get kids to behave. Even today, most people in Apfel sleep with bay leaves under their pillow because they think the plant will keep her away. Snow sleeps with bay leaves, too. If people think that Snow's working with the Night Witch, they'll turn on her.

How could Lucille create a rumor so awful?

She isn't just trying to keep Snow from the Crown Ceremony. She's trying to keep her from the kingdom, the city. From her *home.*

"First, she's *twelve.* And the princess doesn't *need* a curse to become queen," Snow says. Maybe she can convince Dimitri of her innocence, and then he'll convince the rest of the Huntsmen. At least someone will be on her side.

It hurts that people would be so quick to believe this of Snow. What does her father think? Is he worried about her? Is he even paying attention?

"That's not stopping her, though, huh? Maybe it's lucky you got out of Apfel when you did." Dimitri jerks his thumb toward the bright red car. "Anyway, this is where we eat. I'm the cook."

"Aren't *you* twelve?" Snow asks.

"Thirteen," he declares, puffing out his chest.

The meal car is filled with long wooden tables and benches. In the back there's a swinging door that leads to the kitchen, a narrow, clean space, with sacks of dried food, garlic and herbs strung from the ceiling, and a stew bubbling on the stove. Dimitri hands her a flaky biscuit from a plate. It's surprisingly good.

"So how does the hunting work?" Snow asks around a huge bite. She didn't realize how hungry she was. "How are you all going to find Snow White?"

"The rest of the Huntsmen can just . . . sense it." Dimitri shrugs. "They say it's like a gut feeling. Like intuition."

"You don't have it?"

He shakes his head. "I'm not a fairy. They just took me in when I was little. Usually their Hunts are quick. But the princess has been trickier. Their intuitions aren't really telling them anything."

But how long until their intuitions *do*? Snow suddenly finds it hard to swallow, her mouth gone dry and the biscuit lumped between her teeth.

"Cards?" Dimitri suggests, pointing out the window to a cluster of Huntsmen.

"Shouldn't we be going?" Snow asks. "I don't want to get to Apfel after nightfall."

Dimitri sniffs a jug, deems it good, pours orange juice into two mugs. He hands one to her. "We'll probably be to Apfel within the week."

Snow's mouth falls open. That just won't do.

"A *week*?!" she asks. She can't wait that long. She has to get back, especially if Lucille is spreading these unbelievable stories.

It's a little bit gratifying to know that she was *right*. Lucille's been plotting to take the throne. But there's no one to say *I told you so* here.

And if Snow doesn't make it back in time, she'll never get to meet her mother.

Snow needs to get back right *now*. "Who decides when we go?"

"Ivan and Olive." Dimitri raises his bone-white eyebrow. "Listen, Myrtle, they're really tense with this new Hunt. Don't . . . don't push it."

But Snow has to push. She has to get back. She strides out of the kitchen car and around the train until she finds Ivan and Olive huddled together near the caboose.

"*Something* related to the princess is here," Olive whispers, furious. "We felt it. That's why we came *here*."

Ivan protests. "She must have tricked us. Patience, Olive."

"Patience? Have you seen the letters the queen's sending? She's *threatening* us if we don't get the girl."

Snow is tempted to correct Olive: *queen consort*. But now's probably not the time.

"*Shh*," Olive hisses, her gaze landing on Snow. "What do you want, kid?"

Snow swallows a lump of unease. What kind of threats is Lucille sending, exactly?

"It would be best to get to Apfel early," Snow says. "The roads aren't as safe after dark."

Ivan smiles kindly and pats her shoulder. "We'll make sure to get there while the sun's up."

"How about . . . today?" Snow suggests, hoping it doesn't come across too bossy. She's not used to asking for things. People usually tell her what's happening, where she's going, what she's eating, what she needs to wear.

Olive glares at her. "A little gratitude for room and board doesn't hurt," she says. "You'll get to Apfel when we get to Apfel."

Snow winces. She's also not used to being chastised. But she can't take a *no*. That's what Lucille anticipates. So she has to do what Lucille doesn't think she will.

"What if the princess is still in Apfel?" she muses.

"Apfel?" Ivan asks, surprised. "Why would she be there?"

Olive grows still, her eyes looking far away as she thinks.

"Wouldn't that be the safest place to hide?" Snow asks. "Where no one expects?"

Olive chews on this. Snow has no idea how gut feelings work, but she's witnessed the courtiers badger and manipulate each other for years. She hopes she's picked up a thing or two about persuasion.

Olive hauls Ivan away.

"Wait!" Snow calls.

Dimitri materializes at her elbow with her mug of orange juice.

"They always need time to think," he says. He points to a cluster of Huntsmen. "Like I said. Cards?"

She doesn't have time for cards. And she doesn't want to lose a game.

There's nothing Snow hates more than losing.

The hours trundle past as she waits for Ivan and Olive to reappear. Dimitri and the other Huntsmen go through hands and hands of cards; Snow lets her mind drift, anxiously fiddling with the stem of her myrtle flower. What will her mother look like? The age when she died? Eighteen, when she first officially became queen? What will she sound like? Will she smile the way the portraits suggest she did? Snow's idea of her mother is composed of other people's memories, and she's desperate for her own.

And, more immediately, how is she going to explain that Lucille pushed her through a mirror and started this rumor? What if people don't believe her?

"You all don't think Snow White really caused this curse, do you?" she asks the Huntsmen, interrupting their game.

"Of course she did," they agree, and she's too shocked to say anything else.

"Oi!" Olive calls once the late-afternoon sun turns everything a deep gold. It would be pretty—if *Snow weren't in a rush to not be here.* "We're heading out. Get in or get lost."

"Where are we going?" Snow asks.

Olive huffs at her and marches away.

Snow *could* get lost. But her only other option is returning to Edel's, and at least Apfel is a possibility with the Huntsmen.

"C'mon." Dimitri gestures toward the dining car.

"Where are we going?" Snow repeats.

"Dunno," Dimitri says. "Are you any good at chopping potatoes?"

"Should we ask again?" Is she going home or not?

"Only if you want to annoy Olive," Dimitri says. "Are you okay? You seem really nervous."

Snow's annoyed with herself. A princess is always supposed to be perfectly composed. After all her deportment lessons, Prof would be appalled to know she seems *nervous* to someone.

Ivan and Olive fuss with the lantern at the head of the train. Ivan stands on a ladder and pours liquid from Edel's pot into it. Puffs of banana-yellow steam rise.

"Go, go, go!" Olive shouts, and she and Ivan scramble back into the first car.

"C'mon!" Dimitri grabs Snow's hand—she flinches; so few people have ever touched her, and it's a strange, nice feeling—and tugs her into the dining car as the rest of the Huntsmen join them.

"But there aren't any *tracks*," Snow points out.

She wonders if these people have lost their minds.

There's a low hooting.

A lurch.

Like it's shaking off a long slumber, the train begins to move.

"Don't worry," Dimitri says. "We usually don't hit anything."

"Usually?" Snow asks.

But the train doesn't move forward.

It moves up.

11

Rose

ROSE FUMBLES, HEART HAMMERING AS HER kidnapper leads her onward.

"Keep going. There you go. Try and be quiet," they say, because Rose has been unintentionally smacking into walls. They pause, and then the world becomes slightly less dark as the blindfold over her eyes is yanked off.

They're standing in a passageway barely wider than she is and dimly lit by salt lamps.

Without the blindfold, Rose can make out the shape of what might be a child, although the voice sounds like a man's.

"Where are we going?" Rose flexes her wrists, still bound by rope that's getting itchy. "Who are you?"

The situation is almost too strange to be scared. Wasn't it enough to wake up among cursed people? To lie to a queen? To be tasked to cure her own curse, instead of having the help of a proper, trained alchemist? Not that long ago, her biggest concern was what flavors to make her thirteen birthday cakes.

"It is better if you do not know," her guide and kidnapper says.

"I'm not sure I agree," Rose says.

"Mind moving a little quieter?" he suggests again. "We do not want the whole castle to know where we are."

Rose's toes smack into a stair. Her kidnapper doesn't seem to have any trouble navigating in the dark.

Finally, they stop after they've climbed too many flights, Rose's legs aching and her breath coming in shallow puffs.

Her kidnapper turns in the light of a salt lamp, revealing a short man with blond hair. He has a radish-shaped nose and glittering blue eyes.

He studies Rose. "You really are not what I expected," he says, not kindly yet not unkindly.

"You were . . . expecting me?"

The dwarf looks her up and down, the way Rose has seen Edel size up a harvested potato to see if it's good for eating or if it should go to Klaus's goats.

"You do not seem capable of it," he says, with either a touch of anger or a touch of confusion in his voice.

"Of, um, what? Sorry?"

"Do not fight," he says, and Rose doesn't have a moment to figure out what he could possibly be referring to before he tugs at the rope around her wrist, making sure it's secure. This is becoming a far too common occurrence.

They pass through a door into a large circular room carved of light-colored stone. A set of stairs leads to a loft, and the bottom area is consumed by comfortable-looking furniture, a kitchen, and a large fireplace.

A raven rests by the fire. It squawks as she approaches.

"Sorry, Newton," the dwarf says. "Still no Snow."

At his voice, a nearly invisible door at the other end opens, and six dwarfs stream out. Some with long beards and some with short, some with gray or brown or orange hair. Most have small circular glasses that they tuck away in their pockets as they enter the room.

Rose has met a few dwarfs at Edel's. Like Edel has won the respect of flowers, the dwarfs have won the respect of the stars. Even those who work in the mines decipher the stories in stardust that's fallen to the ground.

"That was risky, Bootes," one criticizes.

"Hi," Rose says. "I'm sorry, but I don't think I'm who you're looking for."

"What did you do with the princess?" One dwarf strides forward, glowering at Rose. His gray hair is tugged into a bun, and lines branch out from around his eyes.

Rose shrinks back. "I didn't do anything with the

princess!" she protests. "I don't even *know* the princess." She wishes she did, though.

"Do not lie to us," the older dwarf commands. "The stars speak of you both in the same whisper."

Rose frowns. She finds it hard to believe stars speak of her at all.

"Is this because of the curse?" she asks. "Did she cast it?"

"Of course she did not," the gray-haired dwarf splutters. "Now. What did Lucille offer you?"

"Offer me?" Rose looks between them, confused and worried. "*Oh.* You mean the apple?"

The dwarfs exchange a look.

"It is possible the girl does not know, Orion," the dwarf who had brought Rose here, Bootes, tells the gray-haired one. "It is possible she did not harm the princess."

Rose's gaze swivels between them. It doesn't do any good to trust people without cause, but dwarfs, like fairies, cannot lie. And, unlike with fairies, dishonesty and deception aren't in dwarfs' nature.

"I didn't do anything to the princess," she explains. "She was already missing when I got here."

"Then what are you doing here?" Orion asks. "Where are you from, child?"

That's an easy question. "The Dreamwood," Rose says. Adding, because Edel's name carries weight among magical folk, "I grew up with Edel, making Wishes."

"Edel?" Orion says. "*You* are her ward?"

"Yes. Rose. You . . . you know about me?" Rose asks.

Orion nods. "We have great respect for Edel," he says. "Many fairies look down on dwarfs. But Edel has always been a friend to us."

"Why are you here?" Bootes asks. "Why would you not want to be back there?"

Because back there, Edel had kept a curse hidden from Rose her entire life.

"Because . . ." Rose clears her throat. Do you tell people you have fate hanging over your head? "I'm helping break the curse."

She explains about the potions, the alchemy, Lucille, the apple. Not about Klaus's warning.

Orion folds his hands over his chest, his gaze trained skyward like he can see through the ceiling straight to the stars.

"How strange that the queen consort of one of the most powerful kingdoms is asking a child to help her make a cure. To a curse that has all Reverie trembling in fear."

Rose hadn't considered that other kingdoms would be impacted. Ambrosia, its entire cities built out of sand; Coralon, with its sunny seaside capital; Miravale, with its capital with pink stone walls, nursing its own recent curse; all the small towns in and around the Dreamwood. Are people falling asleep there, too?

But why did Klaus single her out if so many other people are getting cursed?

"We thought we had misunderstood the stars, at first,"

Orion muses. "But the queen consort seems desperate. It must be true. The Night Witch has returned."

Rose is a bit offended. She *did,* objectively, make a good potion. But more than that, she feels a tickle of fear. It's really true. Somewhere near them is a monster, scheming for revenge.

"What will happen?" Rose asks. "Did the stars tell you how to break the curse?"

"Some secrets are kept even from the stars," he says.

There's a pounding on the door.

"Your star charts from last night are late." Amalia's voice slithers into the loft. "The queen consort is waiting."

"Take Rose away," Orion commands Bootes. He turns to Rose. "We are sorry for the confusion, little one. We believe that you have nothing to do with the disappearance of the princess. You will not see us again. Our duty is to the stars. We have interfered too much already."

12

Snow

SNOW SPENDS MOST OF THE TRIP WITH HER head in a bucket. Dimitri tries to make jokes about crashing into dragons, but Snow feels too sick to even mutter that she wishes they *would* crash into a dragon. Anything would be better than lurching through the air, like a sea in the worst storm ever.

They start to descend far after nightfall, and Snow groans. She tries to imagine she's floating in a pool of cool water. She tries to imagine she's a bird and loves this.

They land with a jolt. Snow slops off her chair, and liquid-filled bottles roll from their perches and nearly shatter. Dimitri swoops out an arm to keep them intact.

"I'm never doing that again," Snow mutters, hurrying after Dimitri out of the car. "Where are— Oh."

She knows these trees. She knows that winding trail, nearly glowing in the moonlight, and the peaks of houses sprouting beyond it, and the gleaming towers above that.

They're home.

Her plan *worked*.

The Huntsmen filter out of the cars, Olive and Ivan striding toward the center.

"We'll head to Apfel in the morning!" Olive announces. "Sleep well. Tomorrow, our princess awaits."

As the others kneel down, starting fires, Snow hurries to Olive.

"Why aren't we going tonight?" she asks. "Don't you need to stop the princess before she, uh, curses anyone else?"

Saying it out loud sounds so absurd. She doesn't understand how people can believe this.

"There are bandits about," Olive says, barely looking at Snow. That's why Snow needs the Huntsmen to escort her to the city; then she can escape to the castle. The ministers have complained about the bandits recently, and Snow has no desire to encounter them alone.

Ivan comes up to them. "Don't worry." He misinterprets Snow's look. "We have agreements with all the bandit clans. Although, they're, ah . . ."

"They're still bandits," Olive finishes. "We'll go in the morning."

"You want to leave us so bad?" Dimitri, looking crestfallen, leads her to the dormitory car.

"I just wanted to sing a few campfire songs with the bandits," Snow says, and Dimitri grins. He must like her jokes, which were considered impertinent at the castle.

Each makeshift cubby is barely wide enough to fit a bed, with a chest at its foot. Instead of a door, there is a thin curtain. Around the edges of the car, lamps full of fireflies dangle from iron chairs, swinging slightly. Snow stifles a groan.

She prefers her chambers, their high ceilings, her bed covered with silk sheets and fluffy pillows filled with lavender sprigs. As long as it's not too cold, she sleeps with the windows open so she can hear the distant rustling of the Dreamwood.

"That's mine," Dimitri declares, jerking his thumb toward a very lived-in cubby, a decent painting of a griffin on the wall, a blue quilt bunched at the base of the bed, a pile of worn paperbacks. "We picked up this girl, Marie, for a little bit, and she stayed here. But now that bunk can be yours."

"Hers" is on the other side of Dimitri's, at the end of the row. Someone has put up posters of Miravale's most recent Revel of Spectacles. Snow *was* going to attend, but Lucille forbade it because of Miravale's curse. Reverie can't get enough of curses, it seems.

Dimitri grins at her. "You better not snore."

"Of course I don't snore," Snow says. She can't believe she's here, but—but there's still a tingle of excitement. Because as luxurious as her rooms at home might be, in them, she always has to be "Princess." She can never just be Snow.

There are always servants, Lady Amalia, Lucille. Even though she's surrounded by Huntsmen here, in some ways she's never felt more like she has her own space.

"You can never be too sure," Dimitri says, stepping into his own cubby. "For all I know, you could be half troll."

DESPITE HOW EXHAUSTED SHE SHOULD BE, SNOW can't sleep.

The bed is surprisingly cozy, but they don't have any sheep's milk to wash her face, and no valerian root tea to make her drowsy. No rosehip oil for her skin, no silk eye mask to block out the light. And she misses Newton.

Most of all, she's worried that if she relaxes, someone's going to burst in and string her up.

What's worse? Fairies hunting her down, or bandits looking for a quick payday?

Snow tosses and turns in the bed. She counts geese. She relaxes her toes, then her calves, then her thighs. She sings old lullabies in her head.

But she can't stop thinking about what's happening in Apfel. What people are saying about her. How she was so wrong about Lucille. How maybe Snow isn't meant to be queen, if she let something like this happen.

And it turns out that a lot of people here *do* snore.

MORNING COMES, AND SNOW WAKES UP WITH the horrible realization that none of this was a bad dream and she is, in fact, in a train car full of people who are trying to capture her because her stepmother has convinced them she's conspiring with a centuries-old witch.

This ends today. As overwhelmed as she feels, she can't let a rumor stop her from taking her throne.

Dimitri tries to fetch her for breakfast, but she pleads wanting to sleep in. Once she hears the last person leave the car, Snow pulls on her mud-crusted slippers. It's strange being so alone. At home, people always open doors for her, clean her clothes, hover at her elbow. Being here feels . . . kind of freeing.

Outside, the smell of something delicious wafts over her—herby and savory, with a hint of cinnamon and sugar. Her stomach rumbles, but no matter. There'll be plenty of food at the castle.

At this hour, the side entrances to the kitchen and the cellars will be open to receive merchants. She can sneak in among them and go straight to the dwarfs, figure things out from there.

Snow hesitates. She's sad to leave the Huntsmen behind. It's only been a day, but they've accepted her with games and food and stories, not caring who she is. Like they like her for *her.* No one's ever completely honest about what they think of you when they know you're a princess.

She can't waste any more time. With a final glance

behind her, Snow hurries away from the train and down the road to Apfel.

It's longer than she remembers—Snow's used to a carriage when she leaves the city limits, since it's not seemly for the royal family to be on foot—and it gets more crowded the closer she gets. Though there are no gates around Apfel, the road to it winds up steep cliffs and dense patches of forest. It's *possible* to get into it through the Dreamwood, but not advised. There are things among the trees that deter people more than a wall would.

Snow falls in line behind a carriage full of burlap sacks. A pink donkey brays, and a tired-looking farmer scratches his neck. Snow's feet are aching, and she keeps glancing over her shoulder, expecting the Huntsmen to appear, tracking her down.

Snow is almost at the entrance, a small building topped by the Apfel flag, and realizes she has no idea what actually happens there. Do they just wave you through? Are you supposed to have papers? Proof that you're actually a girl named Myrtle, with no backstory because you forgot to think of one?

But the guard barely glances at her, waving her on with a grunt.

Snow's surprised to find herself grinning. She's not used to people not paying attention to her. She . . . she could do whatever she wanted, and no one would stop her! For just one second, she considers not going back to the castle, becoming Myrtle forever, eating whatever she wants whenever she wants, maybe apprenticing at a bookseller's or joining up with that Villeneuve Trading family, who passes through with such wonderful stories.

But the crown. Her mother. And stopping Lucille.

Snow hurries through the streets, dodging a group of ogresses selling sweet almond-stuffed buns, some witches muttering at a street corner, a boy spinning a sign for a new restaurant run by a troll chef.

There's clearly no curse. Everyone's walking around, perfectly awake.

Snow launches herself through the lines of people heading up to the castle. She doesn't really know what she's going to do. Confront Lucille? Try to push Amalia through a mirror? Rally the dwarfs?

It's all strange and surreal. She doesn't want to have to tell the ghost of her mother: *I was so easily tricked. I so easily nearly lost a crown handed down through our family for centuries upon centuries.*

Snow pauses in the castle courtyard. Her home. Everyone ignores her, merchants jostling around her, tourists shoving past her to peer over the low walls around the castle that separate it from the Dreamwood.

She fiddles with the myrtle flower in her pocket—it could be quite dramatic if she took it out right now. The princess appearing, as if by magic.

But . . . does anyone know she's gone?

She'll start with the dwarfs. Just as she takes a step forward—

Someone screams.

13

Snow

SNOW DUCKS BEHIND A ROASTED-CHESTNUT vendor's cart. Maybe a little screaming is typical. She doesn't spend that much time in public areas.

A man, red-faced, surges into the courtyard, straining against the three guards required to keep him back. Two companions behind him are fighting against guards holding them, too.

"So it's just us falling, then?" the first man shouts, knocking a guard away with his elbow. "Get *off* me."

"What's going on?!" shrieks a courtier wearing a mustard-yellow gown. Snow recognizes her. She was once rude to Snow for not recognizing her family's crest on a set of silverware. "What is *happening?*"

"Nothing's the matter, ma'am," a guard promises.

"Nothing?" the red-faced man bellows. "Our whole street fell asleep. My *daughter* fell asleep."

Whispers ripple throughout the courtyard.

"The curse?"

It's not real, Snow wants to assure them, but something stills her tongue. Something makes her shrink back, which isn't queenly at all, but she can't help it.

"Nothing's the matter?" one of the other men scoffs. The guards holding him back glance between each other, like they're not sure about restraining someone who carries dark magic on him. "Tell that to your stomachs tomorrow, when there's no one left awake to fill your plates."

A few servants, merchants, and footmen exchange worried looks.

Amalia clop-clop-clops into the courtyard. Even though she has the myrtle, Snow still flinches deeper among the crowd, afraid that Amalia will glance around and see her.

"What is this fuss?" Amalia says, her voice rising.

The red-faced man looks at Amalia, appalled.

"Fuss?" he growls. "The curse is here. *It's got my daughter.*"

"I assure you," Amalia says coldly, "we are working our hardest on a cure."

This isn't right. This man seems to believe there really *is* a curse.

"A cure? For who? For you?" With a shout, the red-faced man breaks free of the guards and hurtles forward.

But before he can get to Amalia, he falls to the ground mid-lunge.

His companions slump, too.

Snow stares, waiting for the guards to withdraw bloodied swords.

But nothing happens. The guards look just as astonished as Snow feels.

Because a guard wasn't needed to fell them. They're . . .

They're asleep.

Snow gasps.

It's true. The curse.

Someone has really caused a curse.

Panic sweeps through the crowd. People scream, shoving others aside to get away, but some stay frozen, transfixed by the men slumbering, undisturbed by the pandemonium. Someone should help them, Snow thinks, but she can't let Lady Amalia see her.

One person has the most to gain from making everyone think Snow is responsible for this. From making people afraid the Night Witch is back.

One person has the most to gain from a cursed kingdom, desperate for a leader. For hope. For the natural next queen if Snow is painted a villain and isn't here for her Crown Ceremony. Lucille.

Shaking, Snow edges through the crowd toward one of the castle's back doors, when someone screams again.

Another man falls. Except this time it isn't a peasant. It's a courtier, who has taken one stumbly step forward, crashing into a noble lady and tumbling into a servant, sending crystal goblets of sparkling wine flying and shattering.

"It's *spreading*!" someone shrieks.

"It's the Night Witch!" someone else hollers.

"It's Snow White!" someone else bellows. The fear is like nothing Snow has known.

People race toward the castle's gates, shoving into each other. The stampede topples carts of roasted chestnuts, already abandoned as their vendors flee. A few people drag the sleepers away as screams rip the air; there is nothing to hear other than terror.

Snow's heart hammers.

She has to get to the dwarfs. Things will make sense once she gets to their loft.

Snow turns against the tide of the crowd, toward the castle, imagining a steaming loaf of sourdough, Newton's silky feathers nuzzling against her. The thoughts comfort her as her feet keep moving forward.

But imagining only goes so far. The crowd's too strong.

Elbows crash into her sides. Hands shove her. The donkeys that have carried the merchants' goods to the castle panic, neighing and throwing their hooves around, occasionally striking some unlucky soul.

Snow ducks to dodge a thick arm swinging toward her, but a large courtier comes pounding past, hurling Snow aside—

She bounces among the crowd, shoved this way and that, desperately trying to find her footing, but—

A donkey pulling a cart careens madly forward, frothing from fear, and Snow dives out of the way, hitting the cobblestones with her left wrist. Pain shoots upward.

The donkey rears over her, and Snow barely manages to roll away before its hooves smash onto the cobblestones.

She swallows a sob. It's too much, the pain in her wrist, her castle in such disarray. This is *all wrong*, and Snow wants so desperately the days when it was *all right*.

"Hey. Are you okay?"

Snow glances up.

A girl in a blue dress with long strawberry blond hair helps Snow stand. The girl's freckled cheeks are flushed, and she's wearing a small pack around her waist, plants peeking out around the ties.

"Your wrist!" The girl's eyes widen. Snow can't look down. If she does, she might be sick. "There you— Huh. You . . . you look familiar."

The girl hesitates. Snow thinks the same thing about her, but there's no time to figure out how, because a donkey with no rider races toward them, a cart zigzagging behind it. Large melons hurl from the sides of the cart.

The other girl reels away, barely dodging a melon, and dimly through the chaos, Snow can hear Amalia's clop-clop-clop, and she can't let Amalia and Lucille know she's here. She has the sense that something very, very bad will happen if she does.

Clutching her injured wrist to her chest, she weaves

back toward the castle, more careful this time, but something's not right.

People are staring at her.

No one stares at Myrtle.

That's the whole point of being . . .

Snow fumbles for the flower and grabs at air.

"Curse causer," someone whispers.

The myrtle is missing. It must have fallen out.

Snow freezes.

Most people rush away, but others pause. Some stare at her and start to whisper.

Turning, gritting her teeth tight against the pain in her wrist, Snow hurries backward, farther from the castle, toward where she nearly collided with the carriage.

"The *queen*!" someone gasps.

And for one wild moment, Snow thinks they mean her.

And for one wilder moment, Snow thinks they mean her mother.

But the crowd's eyes pivot to the castle's entrance. Flanked by two guards, Lucille hovers before the open doors, her dragon tattoo prowling over her shoulder, her dark-colored skirts billowing about her like she's about to take flight.

"Calm down, all of you," she commands. "Panic cures no curses."

Her golden eyes sweep the crowd before landing straight on Snow.

Snow drops to the ground as well as she can with her

injured arm, scrambling forward, and yes, there it is, the white star-shaped bloom, a little trampled, but she can't imagine a footprint could knock the magic out of it. She grabs it and shoves it back into her bodice.

Edel had said it wouldn't work if someone saw her, but Snow's far away, she's quite dirty, maybe Lucille hasn't seen . . .

The gold in Lucille's eyes turns molten.

Her lips crook upward.

She takes a step forward.

"Welcome back," she mouths to Snow.

14

Snow

SNOW RUNS.

She runs faster than she knew she could run, racing through the crowd as people stare at Lucille in awe, deciding if they should keep running themselves or listen to what she has to say.

Fear pumps through her, erasing the pain in her wrist, erasing everything but the knowledge that she has to get away.

This is so, so much bigger than shoving Snow through a mirror. Lucille's caused a curse, an actual curse, to get the throne. She's willing to hurt innocent people, the people of the kingdom she's trying to rule, for power. For all Snow knows, *Lucille* is the Night Witch, but that thought's too overwhelming.

Snow doesn't want to think what Lucille might do to her to keep her away.

So she runs, her slippers pinching her feet. They're meant for high teas, not fleeing a castle. Snow doesn't even want to imagine the blisters she's going to get.

Gravity helps her, yanking her down the narrow road from the castle, and she swerves through the city, noticing what she didn't notice before: a sketch of her face glowering from walls, flagpoles, next to a warty, gnarled woman who Snow can only assume is supposed to be the Night Witch. WANTED, the posters read. CURSE CAUSER.

If Snow weren't in so much pain, she'd have to laugh.

The myrtle flower must be working, though, spinning its magic over her like a cocoon, because people give her startled looks, but no one whispers *princess*.

Her blood pumps too loudly in her ears for her to hear if anyone's after her. It's odd, running like this—not to dodge some guards while getting pastries, but for her safety. For her crown.

She can't get back to the castle, so she'll . . . she'll find her father.

Snow's almost at the entrance to the city, can see the path winding beyond it. Lucille, or whoever she is, is after her, the Huntsmen are after her. But her father must believe her. Fathers are supposed to protect.

If her heart would stop hammering and her arm stop hurting, she could try to remember his travel plans. . . .

Guards stand at the city's entrance. Snow can't tell if they're to keep people out, or to keep her in.

No matter: it means Snow's not going that way.

Across from her, the Dreamwood rises up. Here it doesn't seem that menacing, sunlight filtering through oak leaves, ferns branching out, tiny wildflowers poking through the greenery.

Appearances can be deceiving. There's a reason there's a path. There's a reason people only shake their heads when someone wanders off that path and doesn't return—they had it coming.

Snow slows, panting, but if she slows too much, if she stops, then Lucille will catch up. She imagines Amalia's clop-clop-clop so much that it starts to seem real.

And then it is real: not Amalia's clop-clop-clop, but a guard yelling, and the shout taken up by the people around:

"The princess! She's here!"

"Find her!"

"Curse causer!"

Snow really, really wants to correct them—she *doesn't even know where curses come from*—but she remembers the haunting smile on Lucille's lips, the point of her finger, and she takes a deep breath.

Snow leaps into the Dreamwood.

15

Snow

REMEMBER IT'S NOT A GOOD IDEA TO HURT a princess," Snow whispers to whatever or whoever in the Dreamwood might be listening.

Immediately the shouting and yelling from Apfel grow muted, but Snow wanders deeper. It doesn't seem too bad, even more inviting than when she was alone here after Edel's. Admittedly she was only alone for about five minutes before the Huntsmen caught her.

The real problem isn't the Dreamwood in the daylight. It's getting lost in the Dreamwood in daylight, and being trapped for the night.

Snow walks deeper, attempting to stay in a straight line and parallel to the road. She tries to ignore the pain in her wrist so she can think. In a little bit, maybe an hour, when there's enough distance between her and Apfel, she'll go back to the path and follow it to the nearest town.

She's pretty sure her father headed to Mirage, a small village at the edge of their kingdom, bordering the neighboring realm of the Glacial Halls.

The air is crisp here and it will only get chillier, but surely, it can't be that hard to find a jacket and a warmer pair of shoes than the silly slippers she still has on once she reaches a village.

She studies the slippers in dismay. The silk is ripped and stained. The little rosettes at the tips have somehow fallen off.

How had it been that when she slipped them on, her biggest concern was getting sugar buns? How can life change so much, so quickly? How's anyone supposed to keep up?

Birds twitter above.

Birds.

Snow whistles, a small, sad tune that means *help me,* and the birds around her sing in response. But none of them is Newton. None of them does much except make sure she isn't whistling alone.

As the fear leaves her, exhaustion and pain set in. Her feet ache. Whatever's happened to her wrist sends booms of agony throughout her whole body, making her grit her teeth.

Snow sinks down against the edge of a big tree. The

trunk is uncomfortable, but the pain in her arm is sapping all her energy, muddling her thoughts. . . .

Lucille . . . is it possible? The Night Witch in disguise, all these years? Plotting, scheming to take back the throne? Snow had suspected Lucille had secrets, but nothing like this.

Is her father worried for her? Do the dwarfs believe all of this? What are the stars saying about her? Why don't they come for her?

What if Snow has no one?

What if it's not Snow that people care about, but the throne?

But she will have someone.

Her mother, the moment the crown graces her forehead.

The thought steadies her.

Out there, her mother is waiting. And who better than a mother to understand Snow, to see that she would never cast a curse, to provide the comfort Snow needs?

She'll close her eyes for a minute, just to regain her strength. . . .

A BRANCH SNAPS, STARTLING SNOW AWAKE.

It's— Okay, so maybe she didn't close her eyes for just a *minute*. Twilight creeps over her, the sky bruised with purple. The moon is curved like a fang.

Another branch snaps.

Snow tries to push herself up, but pain shoots through her wrist at the pressure. She has no weapons. If only she were good with a bow and arrow or a sword like her grandmothers.

She whistles urgently, and this time the birds listen. One owl responds, landing on her shoulder. Its weight is a comfort but unfamiliar; its talons dig a little too sharply through the fabric of her dress.

"Is that . . . Myrtle?"

Dimitri charges into the clearing, concern flooding his features. He rushes over to where she's seated and kneels down. The owl, sensing Snow's fear has lapsed, flutters away, hooting quietly.

"We've been looking everywhere for you," Dimitri says. "When you didn't come to breakfast, I was so worried that maybe bandits . . . and then everything that happened in Apfel . . ." He flushes. "We *all* were worried," he clarifies.

Snow finds it hard to believe that Olive was worried about her. Probably relieved that she'd disappeared.

Dimitri glances at the sky. "And then this sparrow came and wouldn't leave me alone until I followed it here. What are you— Actually, we can talk about this on the train. We should get back."

Snow feels a little foggy, like she's still half asleep.

"I'm not going back," she says.

She's going to find her father. All by herself.

"Of *course* you're coming back," he says. "You're not staying out here. And you shouldn't go to the city."

Dimitri is also splattered with mud; his jacket is ripped. Had he been to Apfel, looking for her? Had the others? Had anyone else been struck with the curse? She feels sick with worry that one of the Huntsmen has fallen asleep. She hadn't considered the consequences of leaving.

"Look. I already talked to Olive and Ivan. They agreed that if you help out, you can stay with us. I know Apfel's your home, but . . . the curse. If you go back, you . . ." He looks away, mumbling. "You could be cursed, too."

Snow blinks at him. The pain in her wrist is making it hard to string her thoughts together.

"I won't be cursed," she mutters. She's the princess. She—

Actually. Princesses have a nasty habit of getting cursed, if she thinks about it.

"Okay," he says, like he's humoring her. "But let's get back to the train to talk it through."

Snow weighs her options because she wants to make her own choices, but it's getting dark. There are will-o'-the-wisps, bandits, wyverns, brutish cyclops, nasty witches that never forgot the taste for flesh from long-ago wars.

And Snow's hurt. She doesn't want to admit it, but her best bet for survival is to throw herself at the mercy of those hunting her.

"Let's go," Snow agrees.

Dimitri's still looking at her worriedly, like she's a broken ice cream dish. He grabs her left hand to help her up.

Snow cries out. It feels like a spear made of fire jabs through her wrist, up her arm, straight into her brain.

"*Shh*. What's wrong— *Oh*." His eyes land on her wrist. She still won't look down to see what's happened to it. If she doesn't look, then maybe it's perfectly fine.

"It's nothing," Snow protests. "It's just—"

She starts to talk, but Dimitri shushes her.

"Don't shush me!" She's so surprised, she almost feels like herself again.

Dimitri's turned a funny shade of pale, listening to something Snow can't hear.

"Someone's there," Dimitri whispers.

16

Rose

ROSE IS SWEPT BACK INTO THE CASTLE, along with other panicked nobles, into a large ballroom. In ordinary circumstances, Rose would be awed by the burgundy tapestries, the golden-edged furniture, the ceiling painted in an imitation of a sunny sky. But now she feels shocked; the curse is terrifying to witness in action.

People moan, groan, whimper. Healers bustle in with poultices and tonics for the injured, although Rose notices it's only the nobility invited in here. Guards carry the cursed nobleman in, placing him on a velvet couch in the corner. As they pass Rose, she catches a whiff of metal, like the smell in the bakery.

Rose cranes her neck, but he just looks like a man

asleep. Nothing more and nothing less. People avoid him, in case curses jump around like fleas.

Waiters emerge with cloth masks over their noses and mouths, passing out pig-shaped marzipan, jelly-filled doughnuts, little cakes layered with cream and sour cherries.

Rose takes extra, and a noblewoman eyes her critically. It isn't Rose's fault that she didn't eat that morning, sleeping in after a late night returning from the dwarfs' loft and scribbling down a list of every flower and plant she could think of that might relate to a sleeping curse. Without luck.

But the Night Witch cast something like this before, and everyone woke up. Which means it *must* be breakable.

Almost everyone ignores Rose, muttering about the Night Witch and the missing Snow White, clearly all believing they're to blame. But it doesn't make sense to Rose; why would a princess do this?

Rose turns her attention to the healers in their white robes. They've studied a branch of alchemy, trained at whipping up potions to help the ailing.

"You should get some essence of oregano," Rose advises a healer treating a man with a wound as nasty as you would expect from a donkey's hoof.

The healer frowns at her. "I went to the RAA."

Meaning: *I know what I'm doing. You don't.*

Like even with Rose's new dress, even with her hair perfumed from the castle soap, the soil scrubbed out from under her fingernails, it's clear she's not from here. Rose flushes, dropping her eyes to her lap.

She doesn't understand a lot about this place, the clothes they wear, their opinions about dessert, but she *does* understand plants.

Rose leaps up.

That's it!

"*What* are you doing?" an older nobleman chastises, glaring at her as he sips coffee from a porcelain cup.

"Young ladies these days." A noblewoman shakes her head. "No decorum."

Rose ignores them. You can't break curses if you're worried about decorum, so Rose is instead worried about plants. Lucille had said the Night Witch was imprisoned in the Night Garden before she got free. There could be clues there, or similar apple trees, or magical flora like at Edel's.

"There you are!"

Amalia clop-clop-clops through the crowd, and people, even the injured, scurry away. She hauls Rose up by the elbow. "You should be back in your chambers."

"Lady Amalia!" someone calls. "Was she here? The Night Witch?"

"Do you see her?" Amalia asks. "I'll tell you who was seen. The wicked princess. Snow White. In the courtyard."

Rose *knew* that girl she helped looked familiar!

"So it's true," someone breathes. "Snow White is causing the curse?"

"It's a tragedy such wickedness grew in these halls," Amalia says. "But we will protect you from Snow White."

"Can I go to the Night Garden?" Rose asks as they leave the ballroom amid a jumble of whispers, panic, questions—to Rose's amusement, they wonder how to contact that Dreamwood fairy for a Wish to protect them against Snow White. She desperately wants to ask Amalia why she thinks Snow White could be responsible for all of this, but with Amalia, she suspects you only get so many questions.

Amalia frowns. "No."

"I can ask Luci—the queen consort," Rose insists.

The castle halls are quiet. The courtyard is in a state of chaos: carts upended, goods spilled, glass shattered, a few plants uprooted. A gray cat leaps among the wreckage.

"The queen consort can't be bothered right now," Amalia retorts. "Only our most senior alchemists go into the Night Garden, accompanied by guards. Approval to enter can take weeks."

"The Night Witch was there. There might be a clue," Rose insists. "I'll be quick."

And while she's in there, maybe she can find rare flying foxglove, and mix it with rosemary to brew potions of Future Understanding. *Too dangerous,* Edel would warn. If you're wrong by the tiniest dosage, you could lose your mind. Even make the potion right, and the risk remains. But risks are all Rose has.

Amalia peers hard into Rose's face.

"Fine," she says. "But you might as well get a cloak. It's cold among the stars."

She clops off, returning moments later with a velvet cloak that she shoves at Rose.

"Come, then," Amalia says.

They wind through the castle. The corridors are silent, aside from masked servants flitting between doors, out to the gardens, which are swooning with daisies and hyacinths and full-bodied rhododendrons; there must be some fairy magic at work, because the flowers continue to bloom even as the sun tilts down.

"You're surprisingly brave," Amalia says. "Don't look it."

Rose frowns. Bootes said that, too.

Amalia points one knobby finger toward a small stone path disappearing between two thick hedges.

A wooden sign is propped against a post amid some trees, and some of the letters are faded. It reads GARDENE OF THE NIGHT. ENTRANCE. OFF-LIMITS. AUTHORIZED PERSONNEL ONLY.

Beyond the hedges, it doesn't look like anything extraordinary. There are a few plots of dirt with scraggly stalks. Rose isn't sure how you imprison anyone there and expect them to stay put.

"Don't worry." Amalia's lips curl. "The Night Witch is long gone."

But apparently somewhere in Apfel. Rose swallows her uncertainty and steps one foot just beyond the sign.

The world plunges into starlight. The golden sunset is scrubbed away, and the sky sloshes with a velvety black, smeared with constellations that burn brighter than Rose has ever seen. All around her are beautiful white flowers edging a smooth path. There's no proof of Amalia, or the castle. It seems peaceful, not like royal approval and guards are necessary.

She steps back, and it's sunset once again, a few evening birds twittering, servants murmuring in the distance.

"Don't get lost on your way out," Amalia taunts.

Rose feels pressure on her back as she stumbles forward, both feet into the Night Garden.

She backtracks.

Except.

She's on the same path in the Night Garden.

Amalia isn't here. The castle doesn't reappear.

There's a small wooden sign, a message scratched onto its surface: DARKNESS HIDES EVEN IN THE LIGHT.

Unease settles around her. There's no way to go but forward.

Rose plunges into the Night Garden.

17

Snow

DIMITRI PRESSES A FINGER TO HIS LIPS and pulls Snow into the shadows beneath a big oak tree.

Two bandits bristling with knives, cloaked in pelts and bracelets made of wildcat fangs, stride into the clearing, arguing. One carries a small box, and both pace about, kicking up leaves and tearing up ferns. Finally, one kneels and places the box on the ground.

"You have to remember where this is," the other bandit says. "You have to remember where we are."

Snow hardly dares to breathe. Neither of the bandits glance their way. It reminds her of a twisted version of the games she would play as a child, the spike of fear that arose whenever someone approached her hiding place or jumped out from theirs.

"What're ya talkin' about? I ain't gonna forget where we are." This one Snow will call Cherry, for how bulbous and red his nose is. Giving them names helps with the fear. A little.

"You did last time," the other snorts. Snow will call him Claw because of the dangerous-looking scimitar hanging from his waist.

"You was there, too," Cherry hisses. "And did *you* remember?"

"Fine." Claw swipes his scimitar across a tree trunk over where they put the box, forming an X. "Now. Let's get outta here. That fancy lady gives me the creeps."

They stalk off, but Dimitri doesn't release his tight grip on Snow's uninjured arm until the only sounds are the night birds and the wind whispering among the branches.

"Myrtle?" he whispers. "Are you okay?"

"Yeah." Honestly, she's not sure. As she moves, her wrist sends fresh waves of pain through her body.

"Let's get back." He eyes her wrist again, his mouth twisting in concern.

They step out from behind the oak, and something shiny on the ground catches her eye, tossing up a bit of moonlight.

It's the royal Apfel seal, an outline of the two apple trees growing together, on top of the small box the bandits were trying to hide.

They have something from the castle.

Maybe it's the pain making it impossible to think straight, maybe it's the fact that here's *someone else* trying to take her things, but Snow limps over to the box. The bandits have done a poor job, covering it with a few fallen leaves.

Snow flips the box open.

"Wait!" Dimitri calls, a little too late, and Snow, also a little too late, realizes that flipping strange boxes open may not be the wisest idea.

But nothing jumps out at her. No spell zaps her into a frog.

It's just a—

Well. That's a bit disappointing.

"What's that?" Dimitri hovers over her shoulder.

He's so close that Snow can smell thyme, cloves, honey, from whatever he made in the kitchen that morning. It's not unpleasant.

"It's . . . a spindle."

"A what?"

"For sewing."

Snow's old nurse, Sara, used to sew. There was a spinning wheel in Snow's bedroom, and the whirring of the Shepperton wool used to sing Snow to sleep. But then, like Snow's mother, Sara died, and the spinning wheel fell silent and was eventually moved somewhere far away.

"We should leave it," Dimitri says. "It's junk." Except there's a question in his words. *If it were junk, why would bandits try to hide it?*

Snow has a faint memory of an old story with a spindle. Maybe? It can't have been that interesting if she doesn't remember it.

But she's lost so much. She's been kicked out of her home *twice.* Her arm hurts so bad, she could scream. Everything is wrong, and it's *not fair.*

So she takes the spindle and stuffs it into her pocket, avoiding the pointy tip.

"You really don't want to bother with bandits," Dimitri warns her.

Snow eyes him. "They're gone," she says. "How are they going to know we had anything to do with it?"

Anyway, the box has the royal seal. Rightfully, the spindle belongs at the castle, and when she finally gets home, she'll bring it back with her.

Dimitri takes Snow's right hand, interlacing their fingers, as they return to the train.

Her heart beats, different this time than when she was running from Lucille. No one's ever held her hand before. It makes her feel safer than she expected.

Dimitri doesn't seem to think anything of it, hurrying her back through the woods, following a path she can't see. As they move, it takes all her energy to keep from moaning each time her left arm is jostled.

The train appears as if from nowhere.

This morning all Snow thought about was leaving it behind. Now she's so relieved to see it, she could weep.

Most of the Huntsmen are clustered around a fire. Snow can smell burning sugar and melting chocolate.

"Is that Dimitri?" someone calls.

"There's bandits!" Dimitri calls. "But I got Myrtle! She's safe."

The Huntsmen spring into action, and Snow realizes why they have the impressive reputation they do. In seconds the fire is extinguished, swords and daggers and axes emerge, and the Huntsmen surround the cars, keeping Snow and Dimitri in the center. Their weapons bristle outward, at invisible threats that lurk in the night.

Olive glides close to the train, sprinkling some kind of powder, Ivan prowling behind her.

"We'll be safe here," Dimitri promises. "That's a protection Wish, from Edel."

"Nice job," Ivan calls. "You were right—Snow White was in Apfel. She got away. But still. Good instincts."

"Is anyone cursed?" Snow croaks, swaying. Dimitri steadies her.

"Everyone's fine," Ivan says. "A princess can't bring us down that easily."

Snow tries to nod, but she doesn't feel steady.

"Let's do something about your wrist," Dimitri says, steering them toward the sleeping car.

Snow needs a bath, but the effort required sounds like too much, and she gratefully climbs into her bed.

Dimitri leaves, and her eyes drift shut. He returns with a sack dripping liquid.

"I'll be fine," Snow mutters. She will be. She has to be.

"Um." He raises his white eyebrow. "You definitely need this."

"I don't."

Because she's a princess. Because she's going to be queen. Because people always think that she's weak. And she must prove that she's strong.

"Last year, Ivan nearly lost an arm after a rumble with a couple of banshees." Dimitri opens his bag and pulls out some large, sodden leaves. "Took about a month to get him back to hunting. Getting hurt is a Huntsmen rite of passage. For story's sake, I'll tell them you got this while scaring the bandits away." He winks. "How *did* you get hurt, by the way?"

Snow looks at the wall.

Last year she sprained her ankle on a cobblestone. It required bedrest for two days, and all the ministers met, worried about what this would mean for her queendom. Her father distracted them with honeyed Ambrosian wine until they were all merry enough to agree that just because the princess was breakable didn't mean she was unfit.

She thought that's what everyone would think if she got hurt now: that it was proof she wasn't worthy.

"These are comfrey leaves, soaked in a healing Wish." Dimitri wraps one of the leaves around her wrist. Immediately coolness rushes over her, followed by an odd sensation, like someone knitting within her bones.

"Is that why the Huntsmen took you on?" she asks. "Because you can heal?"

He laughs. "No. Edel and Rose make these for us. They just taught me how to apply them."

"I'm sorry." Snow closes her eyes at the relief it provides. "But there's no way a cat did this."

"Rose?" He laughs. "She's not a cat. She's Edel's ward. You remind me of her, kind of. Obviously, differences. Big differences. But still."

Snow nods, but her mind wanders. With the pain retreating, everything that happened in Apfel strikes her.

"The curse," she whispers. "I can't believe it's real."

"You don't have to worry," Dimitri says. "We'll catch Snow White. And the Night Witch."

She desperately wants to tell him who she is, explain what she knows, but the risk that he won't believe her, that he'll send her back to Lucille, is too awful. "Why do you hate her so much?"

What would he say if he knew he was bandaging Snow White's wrist?

Dimitri sinks onto the foot of her bed. "Have you ever heard of the Smithery?"

Snow swallows. She has. And she's worried about what he's going to say next.

"Or maybe you haven't," he says, misreading her silence. "Wouldn't be a surprise. Hard to hear of things that stop existing."

The Smithery isn't anywhere now. It was destroyed

when there was no queen of Apfel, when Snow's mother was dead, Snow just a child, Lucille not yet an idea, and her father more interested in what his cities were brewing than how they were faring.

There had been a terrible chimera problem within their land. Usually, the queen negotiated with the Dreamwood Council to ensure proper treaties, proper defenses for every hamlet and village. But there was no queen.

The chimeras ravaged the Smithery, a town once known for producing some of the most enchantable steel and silver in Reverie, including the Apfel crown. The people were chased out—or worse, the wooden buildings burned to ash. The only things standing were the steel forges, so warped by the intense heat of the chimeras' flames that they couldn't be used or repaired.

"My mom died during the attack," he says. "The Huntsmen found me. Took me in. Royals don't do what's best for the kingdom. They do what's best for themselves. And maybe a curse is what's best for them, this time."

Snow, unable to meet Dimitri's eyes, looks at her bandaged wrist.

She remembers that day. Her father promised to spend the afternoon with her but was called to meet with the ministers. They had to redraw the maps, now that a whole town was gone. One nobleman complained; he had just placed an order for a new ceremonial steel dagger.

A bitter taste fills her mouth.

"I'm sorry," she mumbles.

"But whatever Snow White's doing, Lucille will stop her. She's got the Apfel army, after all."

Dimitri's mother, killed. It's not Snow's fault, but . . . how terrible that she never thought to ask, *What happened to the people after the attack?*

She stares at the ceiling. She hadn't noticed this the night before, but someone painted yellow stars onto the wood. The firefly light bounces on them and makes them shimmer.

"I'll go let Ivan know you're okay," Dimitri says.

She barely nods.

Lucille was willing to curse a whole city just to keep Snow from the throne. What horrible things will happen if the crown is placed on her head? This is much bigger than Snow meeting her mother now. This is about protecting her kingdom.

The Night Witch has a curse. Plenty more magic than that.

But.

Snow is descended from the First Queen, who defeated the Night Witch—Lucille—before.

All she needs is a little help.

18

Rose

NIGHT EXPLODES AROUND ROSE, ITS light breeze, the riot of stars overhead. Plants froth with blooms the color of twilight. Hills roll in the distance. Unlike Apfel, it's eerily quiet in here.

Amalia was right. It's cooler, too, the breeze biting, and Rose tugs the cloak around her as she walks. She keeps her eyes on the flowers near the path, but they're mostly daisies with ink-tipped petals.

Soon it's not just the air that chills Rose. She rounds a bend, and the blooms at the entrance, the soft violet smell, start to fade. The stars become more hidden, like a sheet of gauze has been drawn over them.

Where the flowers once spread their blossoms, tangled thorns explode over the ground, the bramble growing wilder and thicker the farther Rose goes. The clumps are tightly knotted, climbing higher and higher into the air until it looks like they're trying to scrape off the stars. The stalks are as wide as Rose's wrist and the thorns as long as her pointer finger.

Among the bramble she spots shadow poppies, belladonna, datura, vibrant red mushrooms that can misplace your mind, and she carefully gathers a few of each into her belt bag. Hopefully, Lucille will be impressed she thought to come here.

She walks, and she walks, sometimes passing beneath archways made out of thorns, from which large, beautiful flowers bloom. At one point she passes a break in the bramble, where a cottage is planted on a small hillside.

Could that be where the Night Witch was imprisoned?

The moon spins overheard, moonshine leaking off it like sap and dripping in bright splotches on the ground and the glass-like path.

Keep her eyes out for—

She . . . can't remember.

What was she keeping her eyes out for?

She came here for—

A flower?

A flower would make sense.

If she sees it, she'll remember. She's sure she will.

But what type of flower? And why did she need it?

"Look who it is," a voice whispers.

She spins around.

"Hello?"

But the place is deserted.

"It's the little one, come to see us," another voice murmurs.

The voices rasp. They sing.

"We knew the little one would come," a third voice says. "We knew to be patient."

"Hello?" she calls. "Who's there?"

No one shows themselves.

She pauses, waiting for them to continue.

And then she can't remember why she's waiting.

She begins to walk again.

And she closes her eyes as she walks, trying to clear her mind. She—in order to—

"Hey! Watch it!" someone yells, and she collides with something warm and heavy, sprawling on the ground next to a boy in a silky purple suit.

"I know you," she realizes.

It's . . . the . . .

The boy who had seen her in the . . . where? Who had warned her about . . . who?

"What were you *thinking?*" the boy says.

"What are you doing here?" she asks.

"No. That's what *I'm* asking," he says. His eyes widen with concern. "Hey. Are you okay?"

"I'm fine," she says. Her voice sounds like it's coming from very far away. Suddenly she remembers: "Did you see them?"

"See who?"

"The others."

His forehead wrinkles. "There isn't anyone else in here."

He's wrong. She heard them. They had been about to tell her something important. She's sure of that now.

"Hello?" she calls.

"Are you okay?" the boy asks again. "Your face . . . you don't look that good."

"I think I need to lie down," she says.

She has the sudden urge to sprawl herself onto the ground. The roots could rise up and draw her deep, deep into the warmth of the earth.

"Hey. *Hey!*" The boy presses the back of his hand to her forehead. "You're burning up. Let's get this thing off you."

She can't be burning up. She actually feels a bit cold.

The boy unclasps the cloak from around her neck.

And immediately Rose's head clears, like a wind has swept away a choking fog.

She sits straight upright.

"What happened?" she asks. "Why are—why are *you* here?"

It's the boy who told her she shouldn't be here. The tall boy who took them to the throne room.

"I saw you go into the Night Garden. I thought it was odd." He looks a bit affronted as he squeezes her cloak to his chest. His suit seems like it's too nice to be in the dirt, but the sleeves and legs are short, like he grew unexpectedly fast. "You're lucky I followed you in here, huh?"

"Oh. Thanks. I guess." Rose looks around. Everything after entering is a dreamlike blur. What magic is in this garden? But Edel had always taught her: manners first. "I'm Rose."

"I know. You're the one who's supposed to be helping with the curse," he says. She waits for him to continue. "You heard the guards. I'm York."

Sir York, they called him. A question for another time.

Her mind feels fine now. But still . . . she can hear them. The faintest of whispers . . .

"Why did you . . . when we first met, you told me to stay away," Rose says. "Why?"

"Because . . . why are you doing that?" York whispers.

"Why am I doing what?" Rose asks.

"Rose?" York's voice pitches up. "Rose? Help?"

With a trembling finger, he points down to the large thorns crawling toward him, hitching along the bottom of his pants and climbing up.

19

Rose

WHAT ARE THEY DOING?" ROSE CRIES. "Get *off*."

The vines don't listen.

They clamber up York's legs, entwining with the cloak held in his arms so it almost looks as though he's cradling them, like they're sprouting from him. A prince of thorns.

"Make them stop!" York squeals.

Rose stares at him helplessly.

This is not the kind of garden she's used to.

The vines are rose vines. Though they have no flowers, she recognizes the shape of the thorns. But roses aren't supposed to behave this way. Roses mean "love"; the darker the petals, the more intense the affection. Never, *never* has Rose seen them do something like this.

"Try running!" she cries.

York looks at her, panicked, but before he can even lift a leg, the vines seize him by the ankles, rooting him to the ground. Rose winces. She can see the thorns digging through his pant legs, through the leather of his shoes.

"Are you doing this?" York cries, as the thorns climb up to his waist, wrapping around it and gripping tight.

"Am *I*?" Rose demands, but there's no time to be offended.

Part of her inside screams to *run* before the vines come for her, too.

But she won't. You never leave someone behind. That's a rule of Dreamwood folk. Or, at least, it's a rule that you *should* follow.

York shifts, like he's trying to escape in movements so small the thorns don't even notice, and the cloak glimmers in the starlight.

"The cloak," Rose gasps. "It's . . . there's silver."

"Silver?" York mutters, appalled.

Silver repels magic. Knights wore it during wars, and merchants venturing through the Dreamwood wear it in the soles of their shoes to try to keep dangerous beasts away.

Whether that works is dubious, but apparently, in the Night Garden, magic doesn't retreat from silver. It attacks.

That's what must have happened when her mind started to fog. Some reaction between the silver and the garden's magic.

"Drop the cloak!" Rose yells.

But he can't. The thorns have knotted around his wrists, tying the cloak to him. A few of the faster vines have started crawling toward his neck.

If he can't get rid of the silver, the roses won't stop attacking. And if they don't . . .

York howls. There's no way Rose can run to the end of the Night Garden and bring back help before York . . . She doesn't want to think about it.

And she won't let it happen.

Rose should know what to do. She's spent her life around plants, but suddenly that all seems silly, whispering secrets to flowers to make little potions when York is in real danger.

Wait. Talking to plants. Could that—?

All she can do is try.

She kneels on the ground and clenches one vine in each hand. The thorns scratch her palms, drawing blood, and she thinks: *He did not mean to hurt you. He did not know about the silver. Release him. Let him go.*

Plants don't need spoken words. Thoughts are purer to them. "Think about happy things," Edel would remind her when they were out in the garden. "The plants will grow better."

Maybe it's the pain from the thorns or the shock or just how much she misses Edel, and how Rose will never see her again if she can't figure out how to break the curse, but she cries.

A tear rolls down her face. It splashes onto the vine.

"So it is you," a voice whispers.

The vines pull off York, unwinding from his throat, his arms, his wrists, his waist, his legs, his shoes.

One vine brushes against her ankle like it's saying hello. Rose gasps, awed that they listened to her, that she knew what to say.

They curl up alongside the edge of the path, like nothing more than ordinary bramble.

Rose dashes toward York, who thrusts the cloak aside, disgusted. His clothes are ripped, and she's sure it hurts where the thorns poked, but it's nothing a little calendula serum won't fix.

"It doesn't look that bad," she says, trying to be positive for his sake and for the plants. She doesn't want them to feel guilty.

"You can't tell anyone about this," he spits, looking furious.

"I won't. Of course not." Rose has no one to tell.

"If my uncle heard about this . . ."

"Maybe he would like to know," Rose says gently. If his uncle is anything like Edel, he would want to know.

"Yeah, maybe he would." York seems nearly manic. Rose doesn't blame him. He was just about to be throttled by roses. "Proof that I'm just as much of a failure as he's always said."

Rose is stunned. She understands shock, but York is

lucky to be alive. His anger seems outsized. Maybe it's something in the Night Garden, working its way into him.

Rose grabs his hand. He flinches, but Rose tugs him forward.

"We need to get out of here," she says.

Actually, she needs to find *something* that can help with the curse, but though the Night Garden seems passive now, she doesn't trust it. Who knows what else it's capable of?

They don't have to walk far to a wooden marker that reads EXIT. *Our dreams sleep in our bones,* someone has carved.

York tries to move past it, but Rose stops him, clutching his wrist.

"What did you mean?" she asks again. "When you told me I shouldn't be here."

York stares anxiously at the exit.

"Because," he says.

"*Because* what?" Rose insists.

He huffs, but he must realize she's not going to let this go.

"*Because* I could tell you didn't know what you were getting yourself into," he says. "Even without the curse, you don't know who you can trust here."

As soon as she releases him, York hurries past the sign, Rose at his heels.

The twilight and thorns vanish, replaced by hedges trimmed into neat figures caught in mid-dance. Even though night has fallen in Apfel, lanterns paint the garden with brassy warmth.

Rose's heart is still racing, her hands shaking and stinging from the vines.

York pants, his hands on his knees as he sucks in big gulps of air. He looks worse than she first thought, his clothes shredded, his skin pricked from the thorns and bruised.

He glares at her.

"What you did in there . . . Maybe *you're* the Night Witch," he sputters at her, before rushing back into the castle. A door falls shut behind him. At the sound, a guard wanders over.

Rose is flabbergasted. She hadn't asked him to follow her in. And . . . witch? Here, that's clearly an insult. And an unnecessary one. She *saved* him. And left with nothing to save herself.

Overhead the hands of a large clock tower tick. One second gone. Then another. Each one, dragging Rose closer and closer to being cursed.

20

Snow

SOMEONE'S LAID OUT A BASIN OF WATER and a washcloth in Snow's little cubby, next to a clean brown dress and a pair of lace-up boots. The water's gone cool, but Snow's just grateful to scrub herself and put on a dress that isn't caked with mud.

Snow tucks the myrtle flower behind her ear as she cleans, washing gingerly around the leaves on her wrist. They've gone a bit dry and stiff, and she peels them off. She's pretty sure her wrist was broken, but there's no trace of any injury. Not even the healers at the castle could heal a wound so fast.

Today's going to be a good day, Snow can feel it. She has ideas. A way forward.

Snow ruffles her strangely short hair, laces up her new

boots, slips the spindle into the pocket of her new dress and the upside-down myrtle flower into its bodice, and hurries out of the car. But this time, instead of running away, she heads to the red mess car, where delicious scents of rosemary and baked bread waft out from open windows.

At the castle, people rush to open the door for her like Snow is too delicate to do even that. It turns out it feels good, to do this small, meaningful thing. First, opening doors. Next, getting her kingdom back from Lucille.

Huntsmen fill the booths on either side of the car. At the far end is a large wooden table topped with steaming silver dishes. People line up near it. Dimitri, just emerged from the kitchen, sees Snow and waves her over. She falls behind a female Huntsman with rust-colored braids.

"You're still here," Dimitri observes.

"At least until after breakfast." Snow can't help smiling as Dimitri points out what she should try, sprinkling each description with a story.

"We used to buy our bread, not bake it, until we tried to get some from this girl and she turned into a *wolf*. . ."

"I didn't use to make a lot of beans until my friend, this guy Jack, he got this one bean . . ."

Snow walks back to a table with a plate loaded with roasted rosemary potatoes, a sugar bun, and an egg-and-leek tartlet. The food is Apfelian, though different than what you get in the city. Dimitri must have learned from his mother, in the Smithery. Before.

He slides into the booth across from her. Some of the

other Huntsmen smile, but most are absorbed in their own conversations. The lack of constant scrutiny is a relief.

"How's your wrist?" Dimitri asks. To make room for their plates, he shoves aside a few WANTED posters for Snow. It's credit to both the myrtle flower, her chopped hair, and the sketch artist's shoddy job that no one puts the poster and the girl together.

"My mother's dead, too," Snow announces.

She's so used to the buttoned-up formalities, how words must be used as weapons, every sentence a strategy, that she's uncertain now how to just say *thank you for everything*. Also, *sorry about your mom*. Also, *I'm lying to you about who I am and what I want, even though you've been nicer to me than anyone else ever has been.*

"There's always a place with the Huntsmen, if you need it," Dimitri says casually, around a big bite of bacon.

Snow nods, stuffing her mouth so she can't answer.

When you're a princess, it's not exactly easy to have friends. Everyone's nervous around her. And she gets nervous trying to figure out how to behave. Nobody ever invited her to play cards or to study, and she never asked, because could there be anything worse? A princess *asking* to be included?

"And what do *you* think will happen if we don't find that princess?" Ivan roars from his table suddenly. "She and the Night Witch will take over! We'll all fall asleep eventually!" The Huntsmen turn their attention toward him. Olive, sitting across from Ivan, scowls.

Snow's snapped back to reality. She has only five days left before Lucille will place that crown on her own head and Snow will lose her chance to see her mother. And before Lucille does whatever she plans to do. Why do so many stepmothers, Snow wonders, have to be so obsessed with thrones?

"So," Snow says, after swallowing a piece of tartlet and dabbing at the edges of her lips with a napkin. "How are we going to capture Snow White? Because I've got some ideas."

BY THE TIME SHE'S FINISHED OUTLINING HER thoughts to Dimitri, Ivan, and Olive, several of the other Huntsmen have gathered around.

1) They go find the good fairies that blessed Snow
    White at birth. Surely, they must know something.

(Snow hopes they might be able to see through these curse rumors and offer her aid.)

"No," Olive says. "Those fairies are silly. Most of them live in castles made out of spun daydreams, sipping on honeyed mead all day long and singing to themselves. Besides, they hate hearing bad news."

Snow hides a frown. It wasn't *that* weak of an idea.

2) They ask Madame Divine for help, the witch said
    to be able to assist with a wide range of requests,
    even the secretive and unsavory, as long as the
    bargain suits her.

(From what Snow's heard, Madame Divine seems like
she wouldn't believe rumors, making her another ally that
Snow desperately needs.)

"We can't get into the business of bargains." Ivan shakes
his head. "Too much risk."

"Besides." Olive takes a sip of coffee, looking annoyed.
"How do you think it would sound if the Huntsmen had
to resort to asking Madame Divine for help? Like we can't
handle our own hunts?"

They can't, Snow wants to point out but holds her
tongue.

3) They go to Lady Grimm, head of the Dreamwood
    Council.

(And Snow can state her case, and surely, someone so
powerful would see that Snow is no curse causer but an
unjustly accused princess. Not even Night Witch Lucille
could stand up to someone as powerful as Lady Grimm.)

Olive scoffs. "She's worse than Madame Divine."

So that's that.

Snow hides her frustration by nibbling at the edge of a

sugar bun. Dimitri's cooking may be better than any she's had in Apfel, but it doesn't make her feel better. Those were great ideas.

And the only ones she has.

BY THE END OF THE DAY, NO ONE ELSE HAS COME up with any ideas to capture Snow White, either.

Snow and Dimitri spend the hours in the car with the map, where she walks him through the various political alliances, feeling proud that she knows *something*.

Once, she walks outside, whistling, but only a wild turkey pops up. She doesn't know the right songs or the right questions. A bird army's not a bad idea, but somehow that doesn't feel powerful enough against Lucille.

While she helps Dimitri roast large mushroom caps and boil buckwheat for dinner, Snow thinks she *could* ask him to help her find her father, but . . . whose side will he take? Not knowing if she can trust him fills Snow with an indescribable sadness.

At dinner, the mood is somber, people picking at their food.

"What if Lucille's the Night Witch?" Snow suggests, just to see how it goes over.

"That sounds like something Snow White would say," Olive hisses.

"A princess shouldn't be this hard to find," Thorne grumbles.

"If only she were right here," Snow agrees, playing with the spindle and feeling a bit bold. Maybe they *should* take her back to Lucille. At least then she'd be home. Have the dwarfs.

But. The whole sleeping business. She doesn't love that.

The door to the dining car bursts open, and Kaya stumbles inside, waving a slightly stained letter.

"It's the Miravalian king," she gasps. "He says they have Snow White."

21

Rose

I'M SORRY." THE ALCHEMY ELDER LEANS BACK in his chair, folding his hands over his generous belly. His long white beard is flung over one shoulder, and he takes off his glasses, polishing them on his silk shirt. "Believe me, if I knew how to brew something to cure the sleeping curse, I'd be a rich man."

Rose sets the apple on the table. "What about this?"

The alchemist sighs and takes out a monocle, then squints at the apple.

"There's magic to it, certainly," he agrees.

"I've gotten that far." Rose tries to keep her tone neutral. But it's getting harder and harder.

"You could try taking it to the lab." The alchemist

waves to a servant who is approaching with a three-tiered silver tray full of tiny sandwiches and honey cakes.

"I *have*," Rose grumbles.

She's spent the better part of several days in the RAA's vast library and labs. Some alchemists are hard at work in greenhouses, experimenting with different plants and recipes to create something that can wake the cursed, although the nobleman remains asleep. Others are bent over tomes in the library, a breathtaking space—circular, multilevel, with an endless quantity of books. Green velvet sofas are spread out, and ringing a little bell results in having food delivered straight to you.

Lucille has invited fairies and warlocks to stop by and see if they have solutions, but most of the fairies have just eaten the honey cakes, saying this is a witch's curse, a different business than theirs entirely. The warlocks fiddle with their beards and eat the honey cakes, too. Rose has spotted Lucille talking to them, but she keeps away. She only wants Lucille's attention when she has something to show for it. To prove that Lucille's trust in her was well placed.

Rose imagined being in the RAA would be the most thrilling moments of her life. Instead, they're some of the most frustrating, though she still aches to be among the books and the plants and the classrooms. None of which can happen until she breaks the curse.

"Sorry, sweetheart." The alchemist flags down a servant with a teapot. "Time for lunch."

Rose has half a mind to knock his food to the ground but resists.

It would be helpful to have support, but she hasn't seen York since the Night Garden, when he scurried off in his bloodied and torn clothes. She's a little surprised how much his harsh tone stung, and she's felt lonely here in general. All the alchemists treat her with disdain, like she wears her outsiderness as a badge.

Rose descends to the lowest floor once again, where there's a book, about as tall as her, that catalogs every title in the library. She disposed of the plants from the Night Garden, which she's starting to regret, but in the moment, she was terrified: they spoke a strange, wild language. Books, on the other hand, usually don't attack you with thorns. Although no matter how many she reads, she can't find anything about how the Night Witch's first sleeping curse was broken. It's as if any record of it was destroyed.

"If it's answers you're after, you should go to Madame Divine's in the city."

Rose spins around.

A servant holds a platter of drained glasses and faces away from her. "They say she'll help you get what you want. For a bargain."

"Thank you," Rose says, surprised.

"The curse got my cousin," the servant whispers. "Whatever you're doing, do it fast."

ROSE HURRIES DOWN THE ROAD FROM THE castle to Apfel's city.

She's no stranger to Reverie. Edel would knot wild carrot leaves around her wrist for safety and they'd venture through the Dreamwood's secret passages—in seconds, you could step among shadowy pines, then meadows, then swamps, then the Lost Sea, a glittering, waterless expanse of salt that still puzzles scholars.

Rose has barely seen Apfel since she unexpectedly arrived, but surely, no city could be as interesting as the Dreamwood. How could streets with factories and politics rival the Ten Guardians, its ten massive waterfalls that all spill into one glimmering lake lined with pearls?

It turns out that she is very wrong.

Apfel is spectacular. It *almost* makes her feel grateful to the curse that she gets to be here.

Almost.

Every cobblestoned street holds unexpected surprises. There's a small amusement park, where carts powered by magic clatter up and down sloping tracks, and people dressed up as swans hand out bags of multicolored candy. If only times were different. Rose hadn't known how much she was missing.

A few people wear masks over their mouths and noses, but there's an unrelenting bustle. Donkeys clop over cobblestones and street grates, where steam rises like a dragon exhaling. Street vendors hawk candied almonds, a water nymph makes toys out of bubbles, gnomes sell tiny painted swans. In the breaks between buildings, real swans float in little ponds.

It's almost hard to imagine there's a curse or the specter of the Night Witch, aside from a few buildings with dark windows, and the masks. But worries about it never leave Rose. Do you dream? Do you feel hunger when you're cursed? Do you understand you're asleep and wish to wake? She doesn't want to know.

Rose pauses at the corner of a busy street next to a market and tries to make sense of the signs—there are about ten. Some are covered with Wanted posters for Snow White and the Night Witch, although Rose thinks people should be more worried for Snow White, rather than scared of her.

"Hey. Rose. Rose!"

York, wearing a light green outfit, sprints toward her from a toy shop.

"Where are you going?" York asks.

"None of your business."

"I was buying a train set for my cousin," he says. "She collects them."

Rose keeps walking. "I didn't ask."

He looks shocked. Good. He was rude, ungrateful. After she thought they might be friends.

"Look. I'm, uh, I'msorryaboutwhat . . . howI . . . justI-amsorry."

"Okay." She doesn't break stride.

Although it's less striding and more stumbling, since

she always seems to be going too fast or too slow or too in the wrong direction for the people weaving about her.

This is why she likes the Dreamwood. You don't have to worry about traffic.

"I . . . I'm sorry I got upset." York hurries after her, nearly running into a woman walking four dogs, all of which have two heads. "It's just . . . my uncle's a warlock. Lady Amalia let me come here as a favor to him. I don't have very much magic . . . well, not really any, I guess . . . so . . . he didn't want me to train with my cousins back at home."

Rose slows down.

That makes sense. How he acted still isn't okay, but it makes sense. Warlocks train with their families; to be sent away is a sign of disgrace. She knows what it's like to feel like you don't belong.

And, more importantly, she doesn't know where she's going, and aside from running into some dogs, York seems to know his way around the city.

"Fine. I'm going to Madame Divine's. You can come, if you want." She pauses. "And you're forgiven."

He laughs, looking relieved. "Madame Divine? C'mon, Rose."

"I'm not joking," she says.

York pales.

"I was going to buy you a muffin as an apology," he says. "And then we'll go back."

"I'll go back after Madame Divine's." When Rose digs

her heels in, she digs her heels in, especially when she has a curse to break.

"Madame Divine is a hoax," he says.

"She's someone who might have answers," Rose says.

York tugs Rose off a side street and into a little nook in front of a bank.

Rose shrugs. "It's okay if you don't want to come. I can go alone."

"You really think this will break the curse?" he asks.

"I . . . hope so," she admits.

"Why do you care so much?" As far as he knows, she could just leave. Instead, she's trying to memorize what it feels like to walk so maybe she can carry that into her dreams.

"Because no one takes me seriously, either," she says, which is truer than she expected. If she can help cure this curse, she also proves to Edel, to Klaus, to everyone at the castle, what she's capable of.

York's jaw scrapes back and forth like he's chewing on his thoughts.

"Fine," he huffs like a very annoyed cat, but she suddenly feels much happier. She's no longer doing this alone. "It's this way."

They pass bakeries, dressmakers, signs advertising spell casters and transformation magic and wart removers. There are *so many people*. Rose can't imagine what they could all be doing, what they all might wish for, what would happen if they all fell asleep.

"I almost thought you'd left," York admits. "I didn't see you at meals."

That's because Rose has been eating in her room. It's too exhausting trying to figure out how twelve different forks work—really, one fork is enough—and she's trying to avoid Lucille or Amalia, not wanting to admit how little progress she's made.

They stop in front of a narrow storefront. This street is empty and shadowy despite it being early afternoon. The buildings are pressed tightly together, with old, mossy tiled roofs and dusty windows. A nearby sign that reads UNDER DISTRICT creaks in the breeze.

York clears his throat. "You're *sure* this is a good idea?"

Rose's mouth tastes bitter with disappointment. This doesn't look like a place that has answers. But she doesn't know what else to do.

The bell over the shop jingles as she enters. York miserably trails her, although his protests quiet.

Rose's mouth dangles open. What seemed like a small dusty shop from the street is lavish and spacious inside. Velvet curtains cover all the windows, and chandeliers in the shape of seaweed cast a warm, pearly light over clusters of plush shell-shaped chairs.

"Ah." An older woman with silver hair limps out from behind a curtain. She looks surprised, her hand squeezing the top of her cane. "We're appointment only, I'm afraid."

"Madame Divine?" Rose asks.

"Indeed, darling, there can only be but one. However, as I said, you'd best be on your way."

Rose's eyes land on a glass pillar swirling with strange, sensational shapes. They look like nothing Rose has ever seen before.

Madame Divine catches her looking and beams, all her pearly white teeth visible.

"They all had appointments, darling," she says.

"Can we make an appointment right now?"

The woman's eyes narrow with interest.

"My services are expensive. Perhaps that charming little seer over on High Street is a better fit."

York has wandered over to a display case of beautiful miniature sculptures, so lifelike they look as if they were mid-conversation before Rose and York entered.

"Don't touch my things," Madame Divine says mildly.

"I can pay," Rose says, stubbornness flaring. It's not a lie: she'll figure something out once the curse is over.

"Spunk." Madame Divine limps over to Rose. "And spirit. I like it. You're lucky you came today. I'm not very often all the way up here."

"So you'll help me?" Rose says.

"I help everyone. For a price. Fair is fair, darling." Madame Divine smiles.

"What's the price?"

"What's the request? *Don't* touch my things," Madame Divine commands. York yanks his hand back from a teapot painted with small figures that seem to be moving.

"I need to break the sleeping curse," Rose says. "Do you know how they broke it the first time?"

The woman glances toward the curtain she had come through. It moves like there's a breeze behind it. "You're not the first to ask, darling, but not even a king could afford to pay for that."

"Don't you care that there's a curse?" Rose demands. "That people are falling asleep and no one can wake them?"

"Fortunately," Madame Divine says, "I've invested in the mattress business."

"Can't you help me at *all*?" Rose demands. There's no time for being polite. She needs answers.

"Darling, you wouldn't cheat an old woman, would you? Demanding something so valuable for free?"

Madame Divine's not going to help.

The realization thuds through Rose. There's an answer here; there has to be. Madame Divine hasn't said she *can't* help. If Rose leaves without an answer . . . it's her falling to the ground.

When will it happen? When she's already asleep? When she's buttering toast? When she's running down the stairs?

Rose plays the last card she has.

"Then can you tell me how to stop the curse on *me*?"

York's head jerks up.

"You," Madame Divine breathes.

Her eyes flicker to the curtain.

"Why won't you help me?" Rose challenges. "What is it? Are you afraid of the Night Witch?"

"*Out,*" Madame Divine commands. "Or I'll *make* you leave."

"Rose . . . ," York whispers.

Rose takes a deep breath. She looks to the curtain. Something's back there. She's sure of it.

Madame Divine has a cane. She probably can't run as fast as Rose.

Her hand clamps around York's, the other sneaking into her belt bag. She recognizes the plants by feel and grabs a sprig of coriander, grinding it between her fingers. Usually Wishes and alchemy require a bit more finesse, but . . . desperate situations.

Rose blows on the ground-up coriander leaves and hurls them into the air. Coriander means "hidden merit," but this way it just means "hidden." Madame Divine makes a startled sound as the room grows hazy and York yelps. It won't buy them a lot of time, but it's enough of a distraction for Rose to sprint through the curtain with York.

There's the sensation of being squeezed through a tight tube, and then they stand in a cavernous stone room filled with shelves, the top arching above them. It's so large that Rose can't see where it ends. For a moment Rose was expecting they'd appear before the Night Witch herself. She's very, very relieved that didn't happen.

"*What are you doing?*" York protests. "And what curse?"

"There has to be an answer here," Rose says, ignoring his question. "She never said she didn't know what was happening. Just that she wasn't going to tell *us.*"

"What does an answer *look* like? And how are we even going to *find* it?"

"Not by complaining!" Rose says.

But York is right. The shelves are crammed full of strange, marvelous things; they run endlessly. She wouldn't know how to find something even if she *did* know what she was looking for.

Rose drags York down one row, and then another, and another. Their feet echo, and she's tense as an arrow.

"Darlings?" Madame Divine's voice booms around the cavern. "This isn't the friendliest of places!"

Rose quickens her pace.

Down another row, something hums. Rose turns toward it.

"Where are you going?" York protests.

It's just a scroll, tied up with a leather band. Among everything here, it seems the most plain, the least noteworthy, but Rose's fingers twitch toward it.

"How unfortunate if you got . . . lost," Madame Divine calls.

The scroll is something. It's better than nothing, at least.

Rose grabs it.

"Don't touch!" York calls, but it's too late.

The entire cavern starts to shake.

"DON'T TOUCH MY THINGS!" Madame Divine roars.

"Come on!" York calls, but the cavern quakes like the

ground is about to split open, and it's nearly impossible to move forward. Rose looks down, expecting to see a hole ripped below them, but the shaking is coming from the walls.

Torrential rivers of water gush down.

Despite the cavern's size, it fills so quickly that Rose barely notices that her ankles are wet before the water has risen to her armpits.

"We weren't supposed to touch," York moans, and he grabs Rose's hand.

Bubbles form around the objects on the shelves, protecting them from the water. Madame Divine's screams echo so it sounds like there are thousands of Madame Divines roaring at them.

"Run to the door!" Rose cries, but within seconds, nothing about that is correct. There's no running—the water has scooped them up. And there's no door: it's lost below the waterline.

"Is there a window?" York shouts.

No windows. Clutching the scroll, Rose turns her attention to the ceiling, which gets easier and easier as the water raises them closer and closer to the top. The shelves vanish beneath them.

The water rises until Rose's head is bumping against the ceiling. She accidentally swallows some, coughing horribly. York's chin juts up as he sucks in the remaining air. His eyes are wild, horrified. But his hand never leaves hers.

If only she had—

But she does have.

Rose shoves the scroll at York and digs in her belt bag, pulling out a stoppered vial. This isn't how she thought it would come in handy.

"Close your eyes!" Rose cries, unstoppering the vial and hurling the Breath of Fire potion upward.

The ceiling erupts.

22

Rose

PIECES OF ROCK AND TILE RAIN DOWN ON them as the water continues to surge upward. Rose tightens her grip on York's hand and swims them through the hole, collapsing on the sloping roof. They lie there for a moment, chests heaving. Rose feels dazed. Ever since she ended up in that bakery, life has become unrecognizable. And how much more will it take to break her curse?

"There's a curse on you?" York pants. His wet blond hair is plastered to his head. "What are you talking about?"

"We need to keep going," Rose says. She starts to inch down the roof, still clenching the scroll tightly. It looks dry and unharmed by the water. If there is some kind of answer here, it's waiting for her, whether she's ready for it or not.

"Rose." He rests his hand on her upper arm. He doesn't act like she would expect, doesn't pull away or glower or shove her down the roof. "What curse on you?"

"I was lying," she mumbles, because she can't bear the thought of York looking at her like someone marked for sleep. "To distract Madame Divine. We've got to go."

She shivers, her wet clothes nearly freezing in the late-fall air. Together they slowly make their way down the tiles, and they jump to the ground.

From the outside, Madame Divine's looks like nothing has happened. York is driven to action and drags her forward, their clothes dripping as they run.

"Probably best to be far away when she realizes we're gone," he grunts.

They don't stop until they reach the castle, and not even then until they reach Rose's room, although they make a quick detour to one of the salons for York to grab several scones for them.

She sinks onto her bed. If she hadn't had the potion . . . what would have happened to them? York sinks down beside her, their knees touching.

"You think this will help break the curse?" he asks.

"Hopefully," Rose admits. She shivers again, and York jumps up to get a robe and wrap it around her shoulders.

He nods at the scroll. "Then let's get started."

23

Snow

THE LETTER SPECIFIES THAT THE HUNTSMEN meet the king of Miravale near his city two days from now, just before dusk, to get Snow White.

Which is good. It gives Snow time to think, fiddling with the spindle's whorl. Because this doesn't make sense. Who can the Miravale royal family have that they mistook for Snow? She's met the family and the kids—Amir and Anisa—the most out of any other kingdom, since the Miravalian and Apfel domains share the most trade agreements. Should she be relieved? Or is this one more person suffering because of Snow White?

By the next morning, Snow can't take the waiting. Patience is not her strong suit, but worrying apparently is.

"We're running out of time!" Snow insists, but Ivan shrugs and Olive glowers. "What if we go earlier?"

"Believe us, kid, we'd like that," Olive says, her voice taut. She points out dark clouds looming overhead. "But you want to be fried by thunder?"

There are plenty of chores and activities to keep them busy: pots to clean, food to cook, weapons to polish, news from various cities to read, a frustrated Ivan and Olive to avoid, Dimitri to entertain by singing to sparrows so they zoom around in different shapes, and card games to play. Too many card games.

"You want to get all the queens," Dimitri says after lunch when they're still sitting in the dining car.

Snow tears her attention away from the window. She has no idea what Lucille is up to. Are more people falling asleep? Are people fighting back against the rumors that she's behind this? Does *anyone* want her to be queen? "I'm not playing," Snow says.

"*Never* put down a three," Gregor says.

"And if you get a five, you have to slap the table six times." Dimitri wiggles his mismatched eyebrows at her. He can tell something's wrong, but Snow's pretty sure he can't guess what.

"I'm not playing," Snow insists. "I'll just lose."

She hates playing games for the same reason she hates flying: the risk of falling, of losing, of vulnerability. She needs to add *getting shoved through magic mirrors* to that list.

"I already lost twice," Dimitri says.

"I lose about once a day," Gregor says.

"If you lose, you just play again. That's the fun."

It *is* a little boring just watching people play, so she reluctantly accepts the cards as Dimitri shoves them at her again. Somehow, she has seven threes. Somehow, Gregor loses more than she does because he always forgets to quack like a duck when he puts down a six. Snow's half convinced they're making up the rules as they go along, but she hasn't laughed this hard in a while.

FINALLY THEY SET OFF. PART OF SNOW WISHES they wouldn't, that she could just stay as Myrtle. When she's not worrying about the crown or Lucille, she feels happier than she has in a long time.

It still takes nearly a full day to reach Miravale, flying slowly to avoid more storm clouds and dodge a pack of territorial griffins, and Snow spends it trying to play cards with Dimitri and Gregor and not think about everything that could be waiting. Allies? Or a trap?

They land with a thump. Their cinnamon rice milk, a Dimitri specialty, sloshes over the table. Snow sweeps out her arm, soaking it up with her sleeve before it can drip onto Dimitri's lap.

Outside, everything is thick and still with night.

"Why'd you do that?" Dimitri asks.

"Manners," she says primly, avoiding his gaze. But it wasn't just that. It was a very confusing urge to stop something bad from happening to him. She shakes her sleeve and pushes the thought out of her mind.

"Guess I should have seen this coming," Gregor scoffs.

SNOW AWAKENS TO IVAN'S BELLOWING: *"TODAY we catch our princess!"*

Although you can't really wake up if you haven't slept. No matter how cozy her bed is, or the comforting smell of the bay leaves that Dimitri brought her under her pillow, her mind won't stay still.

Because no matter if the letter writer is friend or foe, Prince Amir is so close. And he, undoubtedly, is an ally. If they go to Miravale, she can explain everything that's happening. She and Amir have been friends their whole lives, and he understands curses, how they can make anyone seem like a monster.

And that's how she'll arrive in Apfel, with the full strength of the Miravalian military at her back. Surely not even the Night Witch can face that.

She dresses quickly and fusses with her hair, but there's not much to be done about that. Making sure the myrtle flower and the spindle are close at hand, Snow hurries to the dining car. Waiting for dusk is an agonizing experience, and Snow can't taste the lunch Dimitri makes. Finally the hour comes, and she and Dimitri hurry outside to where Olive and Ivan are already pacing.

They're surrounded by tall pine trees, dark clouds streaking the sky.

Dimitri hands Snow a cloak. It's dark blue, like the other Huntsmen's.

"You're practically one of us now," he says.

He helps her fasten it around her neck, and she tries not to blush. When he's not looking, she quickly moves the upside-down myrtle flower into the cloak's pocket, just in case that will keep the magic working at its best.

"Why are we here?" Snow asks, glancing around the woods. They're still far from the castle.

"This is where the letter said to meet." Ivan consults the scrap of paper.

Unless the royal family has decided to learn how to camouflage themselves among the trees, no one else is here.

"Can I see it?" Snow asks.

Ivan passes it to her.

"This isn't the royal family's seal."

Prof made her memorize all the royal seals for situations exactly like this. A fairy called Durchdenwald created them, making them impossible to replicate. This seal is just a clumsily drawn *M*.

Really, the Huntsmen should know better. Snow could teach them a thing or two.

"How do you know that?" Olive's eyes narrow.

Snow dodges the question. "Someone's tricking you."

Of course it was a trick. No one could have her because she's *here*, and Amir would never mistake someone else for her. But why lie? It couldn't be Lucille, could it?

She'll worry about that later. She just needs to reach Amir.

But how to get the Huntsmen to Miravale without suspicion . . .

"A magic mirror," Snow cries out. "What you need is a magic mirror. It will tell you where Snow White is."

Miravale has a public magic mirror. And Snow's confident it won't work. If a magic mirror could find her, Lucille wouldn't need the Huntsmen. It's a gamble, but by that time, she'll have Amir on her side.

It doesn't take Ivan and Olive long to decide that this is a good course of action.

The drizzle increases, but Snow stays outside, finally tugging on her hood, so she doesn't lose sight of Ivan and Olive.

She could try to get to Miravale without them, but she can't risk getting lost or running into anything less friendly.

"Fine," Ivan says. "We're going. You all stay and guard the train."

Most of the Huntsmen breathe a sigh of relief, hurrying into the dining and living cars to escape the rain. Through a window, Gregor weaves toward a small group waving a pack of cards.

"I'm coming," Snow says.

"You're not," Ivan says.

"It was my idea," Snow insists. She's proud of herself. She didn't even know she could make decisions like this. She can't wait to tell her mother.

"Then I'm coming, too," Dimitri pipes up. He winks at Snow. "I'm not going to sit around and hear about the action later."

Olive frowns, but Ivan nods.

"Fine. Just say out of the way," he says.

The rain picks up as they walk, turning the ground to mud. Snow's nose starts to run from the cold, but the cloak keeps out the worst of the chill.

Olive slows down until she falls in line with Snow.

"Why are you suddenly so eager to help us find the princess?" Olive hisses. "There's nothing in it for you, you know."

That's a little harsh. If Snow *weren't* Snow, then she'd probably deserve something for figuring all this out.

"The curse is impacting my home," she says honestly.

Olive glances at her suspiciously. "You're awfully brave," she says. "Don't see other pip-squeaks from Apfel out here, risking their hides."

"I . . . don't really feel like I have a choice."

Whether or not this answer satisfies Olive is unclear, but at least she forges ahead, leaving Snow alone.

After what seems like far too long, night growing thicker and the storm picking up, the Dreamwood's trees part, and they can see Miravale's pink stone walls up close.

They stop at a large stone gate, carved with the Miravalian Coat of Arms and flanked by two guard towers.

"Hello?" Ivan calls, but even his booming voice sounds thin in the rain. On a hill beyond, Snow can make out the outline of the Miravalian castle and its golden illuminated windows.

Snow readies herself. Once they get inside, she'll make up some excuse about stomach trouble and dart away to the castle. She knows the way. The Huntsmen won't think much of it. And then she'll get this all sorted out.

"Is that—visitors!" a voice carries over the gate. "Do you have your visitor visas?"

"Our *what?*" Olive glowers at Snow. "If you knew about the seal, how come you didn't know about *that?*"

"Those are unrelated," Snow says. That visa must be new. She's never heard of needing anything to get into a Reverie kingdom.

"Sorry, so sorry!" the guard pipes. "And on such an awful night, too! But no visitors are allowed in without processed visas. Have to make sure you're not carrying the curse, of course!"

People in Miravale are this afraid? Has it spread here, too?

"This is urgent business," Olive calls. She glances at Ivan. "On behalf of the Huntsmen!"

"The . . . the Huntsmen? One . . . one second!" the guard squeaks.

None of them talk as they wait, hunching their shoulders against the rain.

Dimitri reaches out and squeezes Snow's fingers.

"I heard what you said about the curse hurting your home," he whispers. "I'm sorry. I didn't realize what this must be like for you."

Snow swallows, feeling even worse. He's the closest friend she's maybe ever had. And he's comforting Myrtle, a girl who doesn't exist. Maybe someday, once all this curse mess has been fixed, Dimitri could come back to Apfel. Maybe he would still want to be friends, after everything.

They wait. Only when the tips of Snow's fingers and toes are starting to grow numb from the cold and the rain is so intense that the wet is leaking through her cloak do the gates creak open.

"I wanted to personally apologize." A figure stands before several others, bearing blue-flame torches that burn even in the rain. "I really respect your work in Reverie."

The figure steps forward. He's taller than Snow remembers, his voice a little deeper. And he's a more composed than the hyper boy she remembers, but after what has happened to him in the past few months, she's not surprised.

It's Prince Amir. Ivan, Olive, and Dimitri bow to him, Snow hurrying to copy them.

This worked out better than expected.

"I didn't think it was fair to make you stand in the rain without a personal explanation. But with the curse getting worse, we can't let anyone without a visa in," Amir says.

Snow's still too close to the Huntsmen. She'll wait until they turn away, as the gates start to close, and then she'll run inside to Amir.

Olive frowns at him. "We won't disturb anyone, Prince. We just want to use your magic mirror."

"I can't let you in," Amir says firmly. "My duty is to my people first. I'm sorry."

Two of his guards step forward to flank him.

"It's urgent," Ivan says. "To help break the curse. For people like Myrtle here, whose family risks falling asleep forever."

He nudges Snow forward, and she stumbles into the light of the blue flame.

No. Amir's not supposed to recognize her yet. Maybe the myrtle's power will hold; maybe he doesn't know her well enough to see past its magic.

"Is that—" Amir's eyes widen. "You've been with the Huntsmen all this time?"

Snow grits her teeth. So he does know her well enough. Flattering. But he needs to stay quiet. The Huntsmen are close and can grab her. She shakes her head slightly. Just a few more minutes until she's safe inside the city.

Amir smiles. "Don't worry. I don't believe the rumors. I'm glad they don't, either." He nods his approval at the Huntsmen.

Snow forgot he could be a bit thickheaded. Well. It's now or never.

"Amir, I—"

Olive's hand seizes her upper arm. In the tightness of her clench, there's an understanding.

"Prince," she says. "We are so sorry for disturbing you. You're right. With the curse, we have no right to enter your city."

"But if Snow needs . . ."

The grip tightens. She's so close, and this is all going so *wrong*. Why is it so hard to believe she's just a girl who wants to get home and has absolutely, one hundred percent, never cursed anyone?

"Olive, please, you don't understand." Snow struggles against her. She squeezes her hands into fists in her pockets, her knuckles brushing against the spindle. "Amir, you have to help—"

Thump.

Thump.

The two guards beside Amir fall to the ground, their blue-flame torches continuing to crackle even on the wet earth.

The guards are unharmed. Which would normally be good.

Except right now they're asleep.

There is a long, horrible pause as everyone stares at them, snoring peacefully in the mud, but the silence is broken by one of Amir's other guards shrieking and dashing back into Miravale.

The Huntsmen back up, except for Olive, whose grip only grows stronger.

"Curse causer," Olive whispers. Snow tries to shake her head, but it won't move properly. All she can do is stare at the fallen guards in horror. Has . . . has she done this?

Amir turns on her, his eyes flaring.

"Get out of here," he growls. "Go far from here."

And Snow doesn't fight Olive, who drags her away, the Huntsmen leading at a safe distance.

Behind them the gates of Miravale clang shut. Those poor men. Those poor guards. Lucille isn't here. The only person who could cast it . . . Snow stares at her trembling hands.

The Huntsmen stop walking. Snow looks up. Olive and Ivan observe her with a look she recognizes. It's the look Amalia gave her in front of the mirror. It's opportunity.

"Skin as white as snow," Olive mutters. She prowls forward "Lips as red as a rose." She lifts up a strand of hair, and Snow winces. "Hair black as a raven's wing. And a preference for some wicked magic."

"It's not . . . ," Snow begins, but she isn't sure what's *not* anymore.

"Don't try to run, Princess," Ivan says.

24

Rose

BY THE SECOND DAY OF STUDYING THE scroll, it becomes clear that no matter which way you turn it or how often you groan, it remains a blank piece of paper.

"Maybe there really isn't anything on it," York mutters. He doesn't have a high patience threshold, but Rose spent her childhood watching grass grow. Literally. She's not ready to give up just yet.

They're camped out in Rose's room, plates covered with crumbs of honey cake and jam-smeared seed bread from the past few days. York is stretched out on his stomach on a rug, playing with the apple.

Rose still has no idea how that fits into any of this.

An apple blossom means "preference," and Rose would *prefer* that things were a little clearer.

"Maybe we should take the scrolls to the alchemists," York suggests. "Or the scholars."

Rose shakes her head. She's not sure she trusts them.

"What did you do back at Madame Divine's?" York asks. "With those leaves? Before we ran into the back?"

"Coriander can mean 'to hide,'" she says. "I made it so Madame Divine temporarily couldn't see us."

"Can't you do something like that here?" York suggests.

Rose blinks at him, surprised that she hadn't thought of that. She digs within her belt bag, finally pulling out a couple of pansies. She fills a glass with a sliver of water from the bathroom and mashes the flowers within it until it makes a colorful paste.

"This could ruin it," Rose says, staring between the paste and the scroll.

"Right now, it's just a piece of parchment," York points out. "Not much to ruin."

And there's no time to waste worrying about it. Carefully Rose spreads out the paste with her fingers, drawing circles on the parchment. Pansies mean "you occupy my thoughts," and she's seen Edel use it to coax thoughts out of objects before.

We leave traces on what we touch, Edel used to say.

Pansies are the best Rose can think of, because nothing else that comes to mind feels right. And with plants, feelings matter.

Slowly the pansy paste dissolves into the paper.

Rose holds her breath. Ink starts to rise up.

"How did you do that?" York asks.

Rose shrugs. "It's alchemy."

"That's more than just alchemy," he says.

They grow quiet as the ink forms a hastily scribbled line in tall, crooked handwriting.

For the birth of a healthy daughter, the crown.

At the bottom is what looks like Queen Elora's signature.

York and Rose stare at each other.

"Is it a riddle?" Rose asks.

York shakes his head, looking a bit sick. "It's a contract," he says. "It's in the Apfel style. I recognize it from when my uncle sent me here. 'For the boy's education and lodging, one hundred gold coins,'" he recites, wincing.

"Your uncle *paid* Amalia to let you come here?" Rose is disgusted. Just because York can't do magic doesn't mean he can be treated like something to pawn off.

"What does it mean, 'the crown,' though?" he asks. "If it's what I think . . ."

Does the crown have something to do with the curse?

"The Night Witch would use a contract?" Rose asks. It seems almost too simple.

"Course," York says. "There's magic in a contract."

This could be fake. But it could also be *something*. Something that Lucille needs to know about.

Rose didn't realize how desperately she needs an answer,

even a cryptic one. Every night before she falls asleep, she wonders if she'll wake up again. Every night she wonders why such a curse would be put upon her. Was that why her family abandoned her? Because she was marked from day one?

And now here's a way forward.

"I have to show this to Lucille." She rolls up the scroll and tucks it under her arm. It's late; outside, the sky is speckled with stars. But this is the kind of thing worth waking someone up for.

York offers to stay behind, which Rose is pretty sure means he doesn't want Lady Amalia talking about this with his uncle.

Navigating by memory of a tour that seems years ago, Rose hurries down the beautiful hallways, past the grandiose murals. The only room of Lucille's she knows how to find is the office, and to her relief, the door is cracked.

"Hello?" she calls, and nudges it open.

Moonlight turns Lucille's office silver, from a bronze orb to a quill perched haphazardly, dripping ink onto parchment. There's a half-drunk glass of dark liquid, a book propped open with a bronze paperweight. Lucille isn't here, but it doesn't look like she's gone for the night.

Voices burble through the room, and Rose panics, dropping to the ground and crawling underneath the desk. She's not doing anything wrong, but she doesn't want to have to explain what she's doing in the queen consort's office so late.

Footsteps pass by in the hallway, not entering.

Rose crawls out from under the desk, peeking around. Her eyes land on one of the paintings of the landscape around Apfel. Unlike the others, hanging straight, it's been shifted on the wall.

Except there isn't a wall behind it.

There's a dark tunnel that reminds her of the one Bootes took her through. At the end, Rose can see the dimmest flicker of light.

Rose nibbles on her bottom lip. Everything in her body tells her to act with common sense and leave.

But common sense is a luxury for people who aren't cursed.

Rose creeps toward the hole in the wall and scoots into the tunnel, stumbling slightly. The ground is uneven and slopes downward. A few stairs have been constructed, and Rose keeps one hand on the wall as she navigates.

Soon the smell of dust is replaced by the smell of dirt, and roots rip through the floors.

She must be underground.

Rose wipes her brow. It's hot down here, with an earthy, overripe smell.

Just when Rose wonders if this tunnel is enchanted, dooming her to wander down it for eternity, she hears voices. The light grows stronger.

She crouches and creeps forward, pressing herself against a wall.

A few feet away, Lucille and Amalia stand in what looks like a cellar, surrounded by wine barrels and wooden crates covered with thick layers of dust.

The conversation continues uninterrupted. They must not have heard Rose's approach.

Amalia stands as straight and knife-edged as ever, but Lucille paces, back and forth, back and forth, her golden eyes glimmering and her dark red skirts sweeping the cellar floor. Rose hasn't been this close to her since that first night, and she'd forgotten how terrifying and beautiful the queen consort looks.

Rose swallows. Maybe this was a bad idea.

"Have you heard from the Huntsmen?" Lucille asks. Her voice sounds like flames skittering over charcoal.

"The Huntsmen continue to search for her."

"I expect more than *searching*," Lucille snaps. "How does a princess simply *vanish*? *Twice*?"

They're talking about Snow White.

"You're right, as always, my lady," Amalia breathes. "She can't be that hard to find. And yet . . ."

"The girl *must* be found, Amalia. Now. Get it out."

"Again, my lady?" Amalia's voice sounds strained.

"Did I stutter?"

There's a scraping sound, something heavy being dragged forward.

Rose tries to peek, but barrels block her view. Is it a trunk? Some kind of weapon?

The scraping sound stops. Amalia pants. Rose leans closer.

"You were smart to relocate it down here," Lucille says. "Now leave me."

"My lady," Amalia breathes.

"Is this how you talk to the future queen?" Lucille snaps.

There's a tense pause, and then Rose wedges herself among the wine barrels as Amalia slouches away from the queen consort. She looks annoyed, muttering under her breath. Her clunky footsteps retreat up the long, winding path.

Lucille thinks she's the future queen? What about Snow White?

"Who is the fairest of them all?" Lucille demands.

"Oh, again?" someone sighs. "Don't you get tired of dancing to the same song?"

It's a *person*. They're *keeping* someone down here.

When, Rose wonders, did her life become so complicated?

"Again," Lucille snaps. *"Who is the fairest of them all?"*

"Well," the person huffs. For someone trapped in a cellar, being berated by a queen, they sound more annoyed than fearful. "As I've said, I can't quite tell. But there is a princess in the castle."

"We've searched the castle, top to bottom, unless there are passages and rooms that I'm not aware of."

"You asked. I answered. That's the deal," the person says.

Without another word, Lucille strides up the tunnel Rose came down, no hint of suspicion that the exchange was overheard.

Rose is lucky. She knows that. This could have gone in a much less pleasant direction.

She should go back. But why did Lucille say she was going to be the future queen? What about Snow White?

She creeps forward, clinging close to the wall. Her footsteps have never sounded so loud.

"I'm not going to answer you."

Rose sucks in a breath and ducks down. It's the voice of the person they're keeping down here. Will they tell Lucille?

"I've already seen you. There's no point in hiding."

"I'm sorry." Rose straightens, looking around. "Um, I got lost. I was, um, looking for the kitchens?"

"Let's not pretend. You want to ask. But I'm not going to answer."

But . . . no one is there.

And then Rose realizes: it's a mirror talking to her. It's in the center of the room, its bronze frame slightly scratched, the glass foggy and warped.

Magic mirrors are rare. Many years ago, a few craftspeople had excelled in the art of making the glass, honing the bronze into a frame, imprisoning a fairy within it. But that knowledge vanished, and most of the mirrors were destroyed.

"So?" it says. "I'm not going to wait all night."

"For . . . what?"

"Mirror, mirror, on the wall, who is the fairest of them all?"

"That's not what I'm worried about," Rose admits. "What does fair have to do with anything?"

"So you do have questions."

"I don't really need those answered."

"'Fair' means the daughters descended from the First Queen, the good witch who defeated her evil sister." Despite everything, the mirror seems eager to share. "Come closer. Let me have a look."

"I . . ." Rose hesitates. She doesn't trust it. But it could know *something*. "The Night Witch. Do you know where she is?"

"Oh-ho, that's a good one," the mirror says. "I'll give that to you for free."

Ideally, he'll say, "Far, far away, where everyone is who's been dead for centuries."

"Why?"

"Because you were just looking right at her."

Rose freezes, the back of her neck prickling.

"She . . ."

She had just been looking at Lucille.

"I'd say run," the mirror warns. "But it's a little too late."

"Who's down here?" Amalia's voice booms, distorted, among the cellar's stone walls.

Rose flinches, but there's no way out, other than the way Amalia is coming.

"Oh no," the mirror tuts, though it sounds like it's enjoying itself a little. "You really don't want to be caught down here. Not by her."

Amalia's heavy shoes clop-clop-clop closer and closer.

Rose spins around wildly. She could hide again, but if you're hidden, you can always be found.

"Psst. In here."

The wall behind the mirror shifts aside.

"The stars told me you might need some help," Bootes whispers.

25

Rose

WHEN YORK SHOWS UP THE NEXT morning, carrying a plate of thickly glazed orange rolls, Rose is already awake, shoes on.

Actually, "already awake" is incorrect. She had hardly been able to sleep, panicked that if she closed her eyes, she'd open them to find Lucille looming over her. The Night Witch.

As Bootes took her back to her room, he wouldn't let them speak, lest they be overheard. He had already interfered too much, he murmured. Even now, her fingers shake. She stood right next to the Night Witch. Trusted her. Lived in the quarters she provided.

"Did you find Lucille last night?" York asks around a giant bite of orange roll.

Rose shakes her head. "I have to tell you something," she begins, but can she say it? Could someone or something overhear?

"Me too. We need to go to the Tombs," York declares, eyes bright with excitement. "I figured it out last night. It's where they bury all the queens, with all their prized possessions. Maybe there's something else of Elora's we can find. Something to explain the contract."

Rose nods. It's not a bad idea. They have a curse, a contract, a crown. Figuring out how they fit together almost feels like a fool's errand, which the apple clearly is, dreamed up by Lucille to keep Rose far from any kind of answer. Of course she doesn't want the curse broken.

They walk out of the castle, and Rose jumps whenever she thinks she hears Lucille's laugh or imagines that she sees the woman's dragon tattoo.

Even in the few days since they visited Madame Divine's, worry over the curse has infected Apfel. Entire streets are closed off with hastily erected barricades. Stalls once full of cinnamon sugar almonds are taken over by people selling necklaces they promise will keep the Night Witch and Snow White away. The only people about wear masks.

The crowds dwindle further as York leads her to an older section, where the buildings are painted white and yellow gold. The streets are narrow, sometimes running in tunnels between buildings.

"What did you want to tell me?" York asks. "In your room?"

"Nothing." Rose shakes her head and pretends to be distracted by a chalk drawing of a princess in a tower. She won't tell him, she decides. He could act differently around Lucille or Amalia, give them away. Put him in danger. Ignorance will keep him safer right now.

They stop in a quiet square, filled only with the occasional pigeon. A statue of a regal-looking woman is in the center.

"That's Queen Elora," York points. "Snow's mom."

She's lovely, a smile playing at the edges of her lips, the Apfel crown nestled in her long, flowing hair.

York brings them to a building at the square's far edge. The Tombs is large and elegant, with wooden doors at least twice Rose's height.

York starts to shove the door open. "So. Just so you know: we're not supposed to be here. It's closed to the public."

"If anyone asks, we'll say I'm working with the queen consort," Rose whispers. Only a week ago, Rose would have had qualms about entering a forbidden place. Now . . . that seems a much lesser crime than cursing an entire city. "There aren't any guards?"

"No one would dare to break in," York says.

Rose narrows her eyes. "What about grave robbers?"

"I guess the stories scare them away."

"What stories?"

He dodges the question. "Remember to be quiet."

A pigeon soars overhead. It's so quiet in this part of the city, it feels cursed.

"You . . . you don't have to come in, you know," Rose says.

"What?"

"You keep putting yourself in danger with me."

He's risked a lot for her. She's not used to other humans, but it doesn't seem normal.

He picks at a loose thread on his sleeve.

"York?" Rose presses.

"Maybe . . ." He clears his throat. "I don't know. If I help out with the curse, then maybe my uncle might take me seriously."

Just like that, Rose feels like she's looking at York for the first time. He wants to prove his place, prove what he's capable of, even without magic. Maybe it's a bit selfish, his motivation, but the end result is good.

She understands.

York opens the door the rest of the way, and Rose's breath catches in her throat.

It's called the Tombs, but there's nothing somber about it. A hand-painted ceiling soars overhead, and dust motes swirl in honeyed beams. Along the side there are nooks with marble graves. Display cases with jewelry, diaries, and mementos run along the center. Amid potted orange trees stand marble statues of previous Apfel queens, carved in such detail that Rose wouldn't be surprised if they stepped off their platforms and struck up a conversation.

And threaded through every breath and every glance of light, there is magic.

It feels like the first drink of water after being parched, or the sunshine after a long winter, or stepping into the air and realizing you can fly. Immediately she feels calmer.

Their footsteps echo, and they read the names written in gold before each alcove, all filled with even more treasures from the queen's life.

Finally they reach Queen Elora.

Unlike the other nooks, filled with necklaces, preserved flowers, crystal goblets used at historic moments, Elora's is empty, aside from a stack of notebooks.

Rose and York exchange looks.

"What are you waiting for?" he prods.

Rose picks one up. The handwriting is beautiful, curled and swooping across the page, but it's just a lot of rambling about matters of state, courtly drama. Rose picks up another one. This descends into sorrowful entries pining for the birth of a baby girl that wouldn't come.

Rose traces the words with her fingers. She wonders what her own mother wrote about her, if she longed for a daughter, too, once.

"What do they say?" York asks over her shoulder. She passes him the first two.

Rose takes out a third notebook. This one is only half-filled, each page ending mid-sentence. The writing grows sloppier, unreadable in some places. Rose flips to the end.

Her blood chills.

If you're reading this, I am sorry. The witch set the curse to get the crown. I did not realize who she was.

But she doesn't know everything. Snow White was not born alone. Find the other princess.

Another princess? Besides Snow?

"What does it say?" York tries again.

"Shh." Rose cuts him off, tearing out the notebook page and stuffing it into her belt bag.

That means Snow has a sister no one knows about, a twin. The last set of twins within the royal Apfel lineage was the First Queen and the Night Witch.

Within the Tombs something stirs. Rose doesn't think they have to be nervous; they can always say they are here on business for Lucille.

"Do you hear that?"

"There's no one else in here," York says.

"Are you sure?"

"I'm absolutely sure," York says. "There are lots of rumors to keep the public from coming in, you know. It's obviously not just a *law.*"

"What kinds?" Rose asks.

"Oh. You know. The usual. Rats. Mold. Magical traps. Ghosts."

Unease begins to drip down Rose's spine. The noise grows louder.

There is someone—some*thing*—in here with them.

"Could it be possible," Rose whispers, "that some of those rumors are true?"

"Hmm," someone says.

They freeze. They look up.

One of the marble queens stands over them, her marble face twisted in a grimace and her marble sword raised high.

26

Snow

SNOW SINKS ONTO A BAG OF BEANS. THE kitchen is still warm from when Dimitri made lunch, but she shivers. Her boots are full of mud. Her cloak is soaked.

The moment they realized who she was, Ivan and Olive hauled her back to the train and locked her inside the kitchen. She came with them without protest; all the speeches she'd planned in her defense withered in her throat. She attempted to tell them about Lucille, but they ignored her.

Dimitri didn't met her eyes once.

She was right. Once he knew who she was . . .

Now all the Huntsmen are gathered outside the train,

which is both a good thing and a bad thing. It's good because Snow can hear the Huntsmen argue about what they're going to do with her.

It's bad because Snow can hear the Huntsmen argue about what they're going to do with her.

"We're sure this is *actually* Snow White?" Mud, the train's conductor, asks.

"Yes." Dimitri's voice drags Snow to the window. "The prince recognized her."

He's crouched, dragging his fingers through the wet grass. The flickering light of the lanterns on the outside of the train waver over him.

Snow waits for him to defend her, but he doesn't.

They were friends with Myrtle. They're enemies of Snow. Myrtle was ready to convince the Huntsmen to rally around her, but Snow isn't. Because, really, Snow's not even sure that she *should* be crowned, that she isn't just a burden on Apfel, on all the people who need a queen. And now she's made those guards fall asleep.

Outside, the Huntsmen continue to debate: Some want to send carrier pigeons to Lucille. Others want to be more tactical, negotiate a higher payment for her return.

"Ivan?"

"What, Mud?"

"I didn't say anything."

"Then—*urgh.*"

There's a thud.

Snow drops to the floor, cowering.

Creeping up toward the caravan is a crew of armed, angry-looking bandits.

27

Rose

THE QUEEN'S MARBLE SWORD COMES crashing down onto the tiled floor with such force that the ground seems to shake.

"Run!" York yells.

"That's probably a good idea!" Rose cries, already running.

Rose sprints out of the alcove and into the main hall, which—

Is a worse idea.

All the marble queens have stirred, holding swords, daggers, maces, axes, and bows high, their marble eyes focused on Rose and York.

Some of Apfel's queens specialized in talking to animals

or baking bread that could make you fall in love. Others favored very sharp, pointy objects.

It's clear which ones stand guard here.

Growling, the queens leap off their platforms, surging forward.

Rose and York duck and tumble away, an axe narrowly missing them and slamming into one of the display cases. Glass shards fly out, and a strange egg-shaped object slams onto the ground but doesn't break.

York yelps and sprints toward one of the other nooks, ducking behind a stand displaying a miniature wheel spinning miniature flax.

Rose vaults toward one of the potted orange trees, tearing off an orange blossom and throwing it in the face of one of the queens nearing York.

An orange blossom means "eternal love." That ought to subdue someone chasing you.

The marble queen pauses, swiping the orange blossom off where it's fallen on her shoulder, her expression tight.

She raises her axe higher and lunges toward Rose.

Rose gulps and ducks down, sprinting beneath the queen's arm before the axe falls, spraying dirt from the orange tree's pot.

"Rose!"

York scampers away as one queen's double-edged sword collides with the platform, sending the little spinning wheel tumbling to the ground. He seizes Rose's hand and points toward the exit.

Growling, another queen dashes toward them, a curved sword held high.

Rose and York sprint away, but the queens must realize where they're headed—they start toward the doors, too.

"Don't you *want* us to go?" Rose yells.

The queens don't seem particularly interested in letting York and Rose leave. Some charge after them while the others stand in front of the exit, their weapons braced, their marble faces blank.

But if Rose and York are quick enough, agile enough, they might be able to get—

York stumbles.

His knee skims the floor as he falls, catching himself, but it's a delay they can't spare.

One of the queens in pursuit gains ground, her curved blade angling overhead.

"No!" Rose cries, shoving York out of the way, only realizing as the sword falls toward her what a dangerous idea that was—

The blade doesn't hit her.

The queen hovers above them, her sword raised but unmoving, her face still.

The room quiets.

York's mouth is clenched tight and he's staring toward the door, where sunlight spills in and glances off shiny armor.

"Intruders! Hands in the air!"

Rose exchanges a frantic look with York.

The queens are frozen, some with weapons poised to strike. It seems like they could come back to life at any moment.

"I'm sorry," Rose tells the guards. "I'm not from Apfel. We got lost. We didn't mean to come here, and then—"

"*Enough.* For trespassing and destruction of royal property," one of the guards announces, "you're under arrest."

"This *can't* be happening again," Rose says.

28

Rose

THE CASTLE JAIL IS UNDERGROUND, AND the air is damp. Even the candles have a greenish gleam that pours over Rose and York as the guards lead them through the passageways.

Lucille doesn't know Rose knows she's the Night Witch. Will she be suspicious when she's heard of the Tombs? Or will she think Rose is still rushing around on a fool's errand?

They pass through narrow hallways, where Rose does her best to not touch the damp-looking walls, and reach a room where a man scribbles at a desk. A lantern flickering more greenish light sits beside him.

"You made a mistake," the jailer tells the guards without looking up.

"We did not," the guards respond. "Caught them skulking about. Up to no good, most likely."

"They're children." The jailer coughs and takes a sip of something smoking. "And young ones. We don't take children here."

"By the law of the queen consort," the head guard says stubbornly, "anyone caught trespassing in the Royal Tombs is under arrest."

The jailer leans back in his wooden chair. "It's all the same to me," he sighs. "Not paid by the prisoner, am I?"

The guards exchange amused looks and then drag Rose and York to a long room lined with cells. It's fairly quiet and empty. The odd person mumbles.

The guards shove them into a cell.

Rose is too busy thinking about the notebook to protest. York hunches into himself, refusing to look at her. They stay like that, huddled in separate corners, Rose afraid to talk in case someone overhears.

What did all of this mean? Elora got desperate and risked the crown for a child, handing the Night Witch what the witch had craved for centuries. Two children were born, and that's somehow supposed to help?

Rose is so lost in thought that she isn't sure how much time passes.

"You're good to go." The jailer jangles his keys and unlocks the door, gesturing at York. "Not you," the jailor adds to Rose.

York casts a dismayed glance at her, but the jailer pulls

him away. Rose stares miserably through the bars. Does the fact that she's still down here mean that Lucille is suspicious? Her stomach twists. What would the Night Witch do to protect her identity?

At one point, Rose thinks she hears the clop-clop-clop of Amalia's shoes, and it speaks to how dire her situation is that that's something she hopes to hear.

"What did you do?"

Rose starts. She didn't realize anyone else was here.

"Hello?" she calls.

"What did you do?" the woman repeats. Her words flow together in the melodic sound Rose associates with those from around Coralon, Reverie's sun-soaked seaside kingdom.

"Nothing," Rose says.

"Me too," the woman says. A figure draped in shawls shuffles forward to grip the bars they share. Rose wonders how long she's been down here.

"This is all a mistake," Rose says. "Someone is coming to get me soon."

"Someone's going to come get us all soon." The woman's tone softens. "Oh. You're just a young little thing."

Rose can barely make out her face. It's dirty, but the lashes are long and pale, the eyes so light blue they're nearly white. Beneath the shawls and the dirt, she could be a teenager or an old woman.

"Here. They'll only go to waste anyways."

From her robes, the woman extracts a small paper bag that smells like cinnamon and sugar.

"I kept these from the guards." She shakes it. "Sugared almonds. I sell them in town. Sold. Didn't have the right permits, though, did I?"

"Oh. No thank you." Rose might not be from a city, but she knows better than to accept food from strangers, especially strangers in jail.

"I understand," the peddler says. "Smart girl. But if you want them . . ."

The woman tosses a few almonds into her mouth.

Rose's stomach rumbles.

Edel always said it's important to eat when you're hungry. And Rose *is* hungry. And the almonds do smell delicious.

"Could I have some?" Rose asks, changing her mind.

"That's the spirit." The peddler shakes a few into her hands.

The nuts are crusted with cinnamon sugar, and the smell wafts over Rose.

She pops one into her mouth, the sugar spiraling over her tongue. . . .

29

Snow

SNOW CROUCHES ON THE FLOOR.

She can't see what's happening out there, but she can hear it. Lots of grunting. Lots of yelling. Lots of sounds that don't bode well for the Huntsmen.

"Any left in there?" Something slams into the outside of the kitchen door, and Snow swings around.

Being caught by the Huntsmen is one thing. Being caught by bandits is another. Snow opens one of the burlap sacks of beans, sweeping most of them out and behind the stores of provisions. She stuffs herself into the bag, pulling a sack of potatoes half over her just as the door swings open and a bandit peers in.

Through the weave, Snow recognizes him. Claw. From

the woods outside Apfel. She holds her breath. If he comes too far in, if he decides to look around . . .

"We should stock up." Cherry pokes his red-nosed face in, too. "Look at all this kibble."

Snow feels like she might faint.

"Are you daft?" Claw argues. "You're gonna waste our time with *beans*?"

"Maybe you haven't heard about that one bean folks are talkin' about."

"We ain't here for silly rumors." Claw hauls Cherry out of the car. Cherry utters a string of very creative curses at him that Snow tries to memorize for when she sees Lucille again.

But she's safe. As soon as she thinks the bandits aren't coming back, she slips out of the sack and over to the window, staying as low as she can.

The Huntsmen sit in a large jumble outside, all of them with their hands tied behind their backs and their ankles knotted together with the rope.

"Which one of you lot is the leader around here?" one of the bandits asks.

Ivan tosses his head back, glowering at the bandit.

"Ungag him, won't you?" Claw commands one of the smaller bandits, who yanks the fabric out of Ivan's mouth.

Dimitri's at the far edge, looking terrified and defiant. Snow's heart aches to see him tied up.

She has a sickening suspicion why the bandits are here.

"We have never once disturbed your kind," Ivan hisses.

"No matter what sins you have committed, we respect our covenants. *Even* when we are asked to hunt you."

Claw sinks onto his heels, his lips drawing back in a sneer that reveals where he's missing several back teeth.

"Kind of ya, ain't it? If only ya'd a thought of that before taking our things."

"I know nothing about that," Ivan argues. "We are honest. We would never take what doesn't belong to us."

Snow winces, her finger tracing the outline of the spindle in her pocket. It *did* belong to the kingdom of Apfel, meaning it, technically, belongs to her.

The bandit sneers. "As pretty as your words are," he says, "I prefer evening the score."

A fresh batch of bandits stroll into the clearing, and somehow these ones seem even more terrifying. They're larger and scrawled with tattoos that depict . . . things that Snow hopes won't happen to any of the Huntsmen.

"We'll take you back to camp," Claw says. "See what the boss thinks."

Cherry guffaws.

"What's so funny?" Claw asks, but he's grinning, too, like this is something they practiced.

"I know what the boss thinks," Cherry says, sneering. "The same thing he thinks for anyone who steals from us."

"Such a shame." Claw shakes his head, though Snow gets the sense that he enjoys this. "And we've heard you all did such good work."

A *shame. Did* good work.

They can't mean . . .

Snow twitches in horror, her elbow knocking into a pot and sending it crashing loudly to the floor.

"What's that?" Claw's eyes narrow suspiciously, and he turns around, staring at the kitchen car.

Dimitri shouts, a sound muffled and garbled by the gag, but it sounds like: "Cowards!"

That's the dumbest thing he could say. Snow knows that. Dimitri must know that.

Claw spins back toward him.

Did he do that . . . for her? To keep her safe?

Despite everything, a tiny flame sparks in her chest, emitting a tiny bit of warmth.

"Get them moving," Claw growls. "Take them back."

"You're not the boss," Cherry protests.

"I'm the closest thing to a boss here," Claw retorts.

"That's not true," another bandit cuts in.

But even as the bandits bicker, they haul the Huntsmen to their feet and lead them into the woods, daggers and axes pointing at them.

They move slowly, the Huntsmen waddling with the rope tight around their ankles. Most of them keep their eyes straight ahead.

When she is sure the last of the bandits are gone, Snow creeps out of the caravan.

Snow is, technically, free. She could run back to Miravale, beg Amir for help to fight Lucille.

But.

But his guards are asleep because of her.

And Dimitri stood up for her.

She can't go back to Apfel knowing she walked away from all the Huntsmen, when they're being taken to their doom because of something she did.

She doesn't want to be that type of queen.

Snow turns in the direction the bandits went, ducking behind trees and creeping through the undergrowth. Though it's dark and the clouds cover the moon, it's not hard to track them—they make enough of a fuss, continuing to argue about who is in charge without "the boss."

Finally they pause, and Snow drops behind a fern and lands with her knees in mud. She grimaces as she peers through fern fronds.

The bandits enter a cave carved into a low hillside.

It's certainly very bandit-y, with sharply pointed wooden stakes in a menacing gate, a few topped with goblin skulls. They're really trying to make a point. Snow creeps forward. There aren't any guards before the cave.

There's no need for them.

In front of the entrance swing three giant logs, swaying like pendulums and covered in ferocious-looking spikes. More spikes jut out from the cave's walls.

Snow swallows. The bandits must have a way to pause them in order to pass, but she doesn't have the time to waste figuring that out.

She's just going to have to . . . run.

The logs swing at different intervals, so it's not possible

to dash straight through them, and they swing too low to crawl under them on your belly.

Between each log is a narrow scrap of space where Snow could pause and wait to time the next one.

Snow counts to ten. And then ten again. And again. Just to make sure she's *really* getting the timing of the logs. But after she's gotten to ten so many times that she's lost count, she squeezes her hands into fists.

She's supposed to be the people's *queen*. She can do this.

Snow sucks in a breath and then hurls herself straight toward the first log as it falls away from her. And just as it starts to swing back, she presses herself tightly against the wall. The logs rush past on either side, the spikes a breath away from grazing her. Snow's heart races so quickly, she's a little worried it's going to fall out of her mouth.

Only two more logs.

She can do this.

The first one wasn't *so* hard.

The second one isn't so bad, either. She scrambles past it just as it starts to swing back, her entire body shaking.

One more.

She can do one more.

Snow waits until the log pulls away and then charges forward—

She's swung upward, the tips of her toes skimming the ground.

One of the spikes has snagged onto the edge of her cloak, yanking her along the log's path. The spiked wall rushes toward her, and Snow fumbles with the cloak's clasp, undoing it just in time, rolling to the ground as she was about to collide with the wall.

Was this a terrible idea? She can't exactly defeat Lucille if she's imprisoned by bandits. But she got past the logs. It seems less dangerous to go forward.

Snow, steeling herself, waits until the log swings back and then lunges at it, yanking the cloak off.

It rips with a sound that seems far too loud for what it is, and Snow freezes, but no one runs to check what's happening. The myrtle flower is missing from the pocket. It must be lost somewhere, in the muck beneath the logs. She doesn't have time to look for it. Not that it matters much anymore.

At least the spindle's still there.

Snow slinks to the edge of the cave, her hands shaking badly as she reclasps the cloak about her neck. Maybe if they see her wearing it, the Huntsmen will remember that she's Snow *and* Myrtle.

Snow swallows. She's dealt with an evil stepmother, angry fairies, and a curse. How bad can bandits be, really?

30

Rose

THERE WE GO."

"You are sure?"

"She is waking up."

And she is.

First comes the smell of lavender and mint leaves, and then the feeling of soft, warm sheets beneath her.

Rose eases her eyes open.

She's back in her bed, a mug of mint tea on the nightstand. Bootes perches on a chair, and Orion leans against a far wall, his face stony. But no York. Outside the window, the sky is golden. Late afternoon. She must have only been asleep for an hour or two. Her body isn't sore enough to have missed a full day.

Seeing her awake, Bootes springs up and hands her two pieces of rosemary bread wrapped in a tea towel.

"Our brothers baked this for you," he says. "They thought it might make you feel better."

She's touched, but confused. She was expecting slimy walls, not fresh bread. "What's going on? How did I— I was in prison."

"You were," Orion agrees.

"But not anymore," Bootes says.

"The almonds," Rose realizes.

"Poisoned," Orion says.

"But you are fine," Bootes hurries to say.

Rose feels a little queasy, but nothing more. It seems like the almonds weren't meant to hurt her permanently. Just knock her out.

"The guards brought you back," Bootes says. "After you collapsed. But the stars told us. And we thought you might want to wake up to a friendly face."

"Why would that woman poison me?" Rose asks.

"We could get in great trouble for interfering in human affairs," Orion says, gesturing toward their hole in the wall.

"You're interfering now," Rose points out. "Please. Tell me."

"We . . . ," Bootes begins. Orion shakes his head, but Bootes barrels on. "We think it was the queen consort. In disguise."

The thought is chilling.

"You know who she is," Rose realizes. Otherwise, why

suspect her? "How long? How long have you known she's the Night Witch?"

Bootes won't meet Rose's eyes.

"It is not our duty to interfere in human affairs," Orion says gruffly. "And sometimes we may misread the stars. It did not seem like it could be true, when they said the Night Witch had been among us for so long."

Rose feels a rush of frustration at them, followed by confusion. If Lucille wanted to poison her, Rose has the feeling she would already be dead.

Unless . . .

She nearly drops the teacup, shoving it onto the nightstand to turn her belt bag and pockets inside out.

It's gone.

The note from Queen Elora's notebook. The note about the lost princess.

Lucille has it. Lucille knows.

Whoever this lost princess is, she'll be in danger.

Rose hurriedly explains the contract and the note. The dwarfs listen and exchange pointed looks after nearly every sentence.

When Rose finishes speaking, neither dwarf seems surprised. It's as if they knew all this already, from the stars or the royal family, or simply by observing.

"We think we understand why the stars spoke of you and Snow together," Bootes whispers. Rose wraps the blanket tighter around herself, suddenly chilled.

"Bootes," Orion warns.

"Orion," Bootes counters. "Perhaps it is time we share what the stars have said."

Rose expects Orion to put up more of a fuss, but instead he stares out the window. His words come out low and quiet, like dusk.

"Queen Elora gave birth to two daughters, not just Snow White," he says. "As was the custom, Elora alone was there when the fairies gave their blessings. Perhaps even then she suspected something was wrong, because she hid one baby behind a curtain, alternating each time, so the blessings would be spread. And no one would know there were two princesses."

"So the Night Witch wouldn't find out," Rose murmurs.

Orion nods. "We did not know about the contract. But now I understand. The First Queen, Nora, placed many enchantments to keep the Night Witch from the throne, including making her unable to harm a princess of Apfel or wear the crown while a princess was fit to become queen. But the contract allowed her to harm the child. Cursed and asleep, the girl would not be fit to take the throne, and there would be nothing between the Night Witch and the crown. But the Night Witch does not know about the second girl. We believe she knows only that Snow White is cursed to fall asleep, and she assumes that at the Crown Ceremony, she will be free to assume power once again."

Except now Lucille has Elora's notebook. Now she knows about the other girl.

Rose shivers. "What happened to the second daughter?"

"She was taken to safety in the Dreamwood to be raised by a good fairy. Elora didn't tell anyone else of the curse before she died."

The hairs on the back of Rose's neck stand up. There are many good fairies. But what Klaus said . . . Never mind that. That's preposterous.

"How can we break the sleeping curse?" Rose asks. She can't defeat the Night Witch. But ending the curse could help. "How did the First Queen do it?"

"We do not know exactly." Orion tugs on his beard, looking pained to be sharing the stars' secrets. "But we do know that the other princess is at the castle. And the stars think she can help break the curse."

He looks at her and raises his eyebrows.

"So what? What are you saying?" Rose pleads. She swings her legs off the bed. She thinks she . . . They can't possibly mean . . . That would be *impossible.*

"You . . . ," Bootes starts.

Someone bangs on the door. The dwarfs rush into the walls, the panel closing seamlessly behind them.

"It's me, Rose," York calls. "I think I found something."

31

Snow

I N THE TIME IT TAKES SNOW TO GET PAST THE logs, she loses sight of the bandits. Which wouldn't seem like it would be an issue in a cave, except that this cave is more a sprawling maze.

Tunnels spurt off to mysterious ends. There are bandit pubs and bandit gathering halls, bandit bedrooms and bandit wrestling pits, stinky stables with rare six-legged horses—that must be how Claw and Cherry made it so quickly from Apfel to Miravale. Snow drifts forward, the cloak pulled over her head as people rush past, sharpen weapons, sing, clip her on the shoulders and tell her to *watch it, mutt.* Snow stops herself before trodding on one of them, sprawled asleep on the ground.

Luckily, the tunnels are crowded enough that only a parrot in a cage made out of bones pays her any attention. "Just your voice!" it cries. "Just your voice!"

"I think I'll keep it, thanks," Snow mutters, although she's always been a little self-conscious about her voice. That fairy who was supposed to have given her a honeyed voice could have tried harder with her blessing.

All concerns about her singing evaporate as the tunnel widens into a large cavern. There are rusted structures used for storage and a carcass of a massive sailing ship. Clustered in the center: the Huntsmen. A few of the bandits are still shoving the fairies into place, their laughter like nails screeching down a blackboard.

Snow scoots underneath one of the metal shelves, the shadows crisscrossing over her.

"Got 'em, boss," Cherry says.

A man detaches from the shadows, and Snow prickles with goose bumps. She wonders how many other bandits lurk unseen in the dark. The fear she feels is worse than the fear of flying, of humiliation, of being seen as weak, but she has to go forward, move with the fear, rather than against it.

The man is short, with dark hair slicked back and a swagger that reminds Snow of a wizard she once met who carried power like he had done unspeakable things to earn it.

"Dogtooth," Ivan growls.

"Ivan." Dogtooth smiles. When he speaks, Snow flinches. His canine teeth are three times the length and double the size of a normal person's, and completely black.

"I see you got our letter from the royal family," Dogtooth continues. "Not a bad trick to get you here, no? Timber's learning calligraphy."

"Let us go," Ivan says. "This has to be a mistake."

For once Olive is silent, her face ashen. Seeing Olive afraid makes the situation seem much, much worse.

"Ah, how I wish it was," Dogtooth says, spreading his arms wide. "I always told you it was better to be on my good side."

"We've done nothing to be on your bad side," Ivan argues, struggling against the ropes. Snow winces.

Dogtooth tilts his head, his eyes crinkling.

"You missed one," he says.

"That's not my fault," Claw is quick to say. "Wait. Whaddya mean, we missed one?"

Dogtooth extends one squat finger, leering at Snow, who feels her stomach plop down alongside her feet. She thought she was hidden.

"Don't be shy, sweetheart," he says. "Nobody likes a wallflower."

Snow *would* have stepped forward boldly, but the bandits get to her first, two bolting out of the shadows and dragging her toward the Huntsmen. Their hands are tight clamps on her upper arms.

Ivan swears under his breath. Olive's nostrils flare.

"Myrt—Snow White," Dimitri breathes. "What are you doing here?"

"I'm here to rescue you," Snow declares, annoyed at how her voice trembles. She was supposed to sound queenly. Instead, she sounds like someone who barely dodged some swinging logs.

"You could have got away," Olive whispers.

Dimitri stares at her, his eyes narrowed.

"Release her," Dogtooth commands.

"What?" Claw asks.

"What?" Snow asks.

"Don't you know who this is?" Dogtooth asks, gesturing for the guards to free her. Reluctantly, they step away from Snow.

The corner of Dogtooth's mouth twitches, and he bows deeply.

"Welcome, Princess," he says.

32

Rose

ROSE IGNORES THE DOOR AND TAPS ON THE wall.

"Bootes," she whispers. "Me what?"

Silence.

"Bootes," she whispers. "Which good fairy?"

She doesn't expect them to return, but then she hears Bootes's whisper: "The Fairy of Flora." He coughs. "I believe you know her, Princess."

Rose stares at the wall, surprised she doesn't fall over.

If someone had told her she was related to a family of crows, she'd be less surprised. *Her?* No. She loves soil and plants and has avoided every full castle meal because she can't figure out which fork to use.

York pounds on the door again.

She's the one who's meant to fall asleep, not Snow White, like Lucille thinks. But she's supposed to have some role in breaking the curse? Believe her. She's *tried*.

"Rose!" York calls, and it drags her to the door. She cracks it open.

"Rose? Are you okay?"

In the hours since leaving the prison, York has scrubbed and changed. He still looks shaken, though, and a bruise blooms on his cheek.

"Yeah," she says, her mouth feeling strange.

It could be a coincidence. A cursed princess. Taken to the woods by a good fairy. The dwarfs could be wrong.

But . . . what good does this do her now? *She* can't break the curse. She has absolutely no idea what to do. And tomorrow . . . her birthday. The Crown Ceremony. The end of everything the Night Witch has set in motion.

"I think I found something," he says. "Something that can break the curse."

33

Snow

HOW LUCKY WE ARE TO HAVE SUCH AN honored guest." Dogtooth remains in a bow. "It's been a long time since a queen of Apfel has set foot in our humble halls."

Snow grins. This is better than she could have hoped.

They don't just know who she is. *Here* are allies. She had no idea that queens of Apfel were friends with bandits, but that's a matter for another time.

"Yes. Well. You're welcome." Snow stands up straighter, throwing her shoulders back, as a queen probably does. "Now. Free them. We have a much larger problem in front of us."

Snow may be ragged from the rain and mud. Her cloak might be nearly shredded, and she may smell like sweat and dirt. She may be talking to a crowd of bandits. But they regard her as the future queen.

And then she can free the Huntsmen and prove to them that she's not the evil, curse-casting princess they believe she is.

"You're free to go." Dogtooth straightens, baring his black canines. "Your grandmother did my grandfather a kindness many years ago. The Ironhall Bandits have since sworn dedication to the queens of Apfel. We hope that you will remember our friendship once you take the throne."

"And so I shall," Snow declares, because she thinks this is something her mother might say. She begins to trot away, but the only footsteps she hears are her own.

The Huntsmen aren't following.

She turns. They're still huddled together, the bandits' rusty weapons shoved at them. Dimitri shakes his head at her.

"You're letting them go, too," Snow reminds Dogtooth.

Dogtooth considers this, and then frowns.

"Oh, Princess. You must understand. Life in the Wood requires a balance. Debts must be repaid."

"Well, um, repay it another way," she suggests. "I'm not leaving without them."

Her fingers twitch to the spindle. She could return it. But she has a creeping sense that's not going to do any good now. . . .

"Really?" Dogtooth eyes her. "That's your decision?"

"I leave when they leave," Snow declares.

Dogtooth sighs. "I wish you hadn't said that."

Dogtooth's gesture is subtle, but the guards storm her, wrenching her hands behind her back, tying them with thick rope, and shoving her among the Huntsmen. Dimitri is on the other side; she can't see him.

This isn't how Snow expected things to go.

"What about our grandparents?" she gasps. She's the future queen; he said so. He should want to be on her good side.

Unless he's not worried about her having any sides after this.

"Yes." Dogtooth scratches the back of his neck. "That's too bad. But you're not your grandmother, and I'm not my grandfather, and we can revisit that agreement next time we happen to run into each other. Unfortunately"—he sighs, like all this is out of his control—"that time may never come."

"But I'm the princess!" Snow cries, shocked. He can't possibly intend to hurt a princess.

"And there'll be no one to tell what happened to you." Dogtooth twitches his fingers toward a passageway.

The rest of the bandits glance at each other.

"You're . . . uh, you're sure that's what you want to do there, boss?" Cherry asks.

"Yes. Just like I want to do this."

Snow barely even sees him clench his fingers before a bandit with bright green tattoos strikes Cherry to the ground.

"*Don't* disagree with me," Dogtooth spits. It's highly possible Snow made a mistake by not escaping when she could.

The rest of the bandits fall silent, faces drawn in grim concentration, as they haul the Huntsmen, Snow among them, into another cavern. This one has a large pit in the middle, where darkness swirls.

Claw delights in shoving Snow a little harder. The rope chafes against her wrists.

"You shouldn't have done that," Ivan whispers to Snow. She can't read his expression: it's either anger or regret. "No one's going to remember that you came back for us."

His reaction stings; does he not understand what they all mean to her?

"You will," she promises. "And you can tell everyone else about it after we get out of here."

They're not going to die in an old cave, and neither is she. That would make Lucille far too happy.

Everyone pauses near the pit.

Even Dogtooth looks a little unnerved. He tugs at the neck of his shirt.

"Rise, great beast," he commands. "Rise and find your quarry."

Olive swears.

Dimitri looks petrified. Some of the Huntsmen squeeze their eyes shut, maybe praying.

Snow feels guilty, but there is still a part of her that is overwhelmingly sure that, somehow, giving the bandits the spindle would be a terrible idea.

Nothing seems to rise.

But then there's a deep groan, and from the pit emerges a pair of giant black spikes and the tips of impossibly large wings.

The fear that Snow has been trying to push down soars up, and the ground feels like it's tilting beneath her.

Rising from the pit is a dragon.

34

Snow

THE DRAGON HAULS ITSELF UPWARD, landing with an earthquaking thump on the ground beside Dogtooth. Its eyes are tightly bound by red cloth.

But—it's not a dragon at all.

In terms of its size and its fierceness, though, it makes little difference.

Snow recognizes it from Prof's lessons.

It's a cockatrice, a massive creature at least three tall people long. It has the head, plumage, and beak of a rooster and the body of a feathered wyvern, with two great wings and two legs ending in reptilian claws. Cockatrices are rare, dwelling in swampy areas that are usually flooded with other dangerous creatures. The alchemists at the castle are always eager for cockatrice blood, but it's hard to track down and even harder to bottle before its magic dissolves into the air.

Magic that . . .

That might make a dragon a little more preferable.

It squawks, and all the Huntsmen cower. Dogtooth pulls a bell from inside his vest. When he rings it, the cockatrice quiets.

It's terrified, Snow realizes. Just like them. It doesn't want to be underground. It doesn't want its eyes covered.

But if its eyes aren't covered, anyone who meets its gaze will be turned to stone, frozen for eternity. And it's hard to keep your eyes closed when a cockatrice is breathing gusts of fire at you. Dragons, at least, you can run from with your eyes open.

"Come, you massive swine," Dogtooth commands, clicking his tongue against his teeth.

The cockatrice sways closer and closer, its long scaly body unspooling behind it like thread. It's at least two Dimitris in width. Even the strongest and brawniest of the Huntsmen tremble as it approaches. Dogtooth grins, shaking the little bell even harder.

"Please," Ivan grunts, nearly begging. Snow doesn't blame him. "Please."

"Try to make your last words good," Dogtooth encourages. "Maybe one of us will be in a fair enough mood to write them down."

Snow can't get back to her throne if she's little better than a statue.

"Out of the way, boys!" Dogtooth declares. The bandits step aside, looking like they'd rather flee. A few Huntsmen squeeze their eyes shut, but more only squint, as if they'll be able to dodge any flames that billow from the cockatrice's beak.

Snow's not afraid anymore. Is she just numb, resigned to her fate? Too angry to feel fear?

The cockatrice growls. And Snow realizes she's hearing something the others aren't.

It's like with Newton, and the pigeons in the castle courtyard, and the falcons in the Dreamwood. She can understand it.

The cockatrice is frightened of the dark and of being harmed by the bandits, but it doesn't want to hurt them.

Snow squeezes her fists so tight that her nails sting her palms.

And then she starts to whistle.

It's an old song, one that Sara, her nurse, said her mother used to sing.

Cockatrices have bird ancestry, she's sure. Didn't Prof say something like that?

Listening to Snow, the cockatrice turns its face from the Huntsmen and straight toward Dogtooth. Its long tail snakes toward him.

Dogtooth licks his lips and rubs his palms together.

"Stop that, boys," he calls out, sounding uncertain. "Now's not the time for jokes."

Snow keeps whistling. She's a little bit worried that she'll lose the tune, that this isn't the right song, but the cockatrice listens.

"Who's doing that? Is that you, Humphrey?" Dogtooth demands. "Stop it, or to the pit with you!"

There's a cough as Snow keeps whistling. All the bandits keep backing away. Finally one mutters, "Not me, boss."

"I've— Enough with this!" Dogtooth roars, tearing the blindfold off the cockatrice.

The Huntsmen scream in anticipation of eternal petrification and—

They remain unpetrified.

The cockatrice sways, its eyes closed, listening to Snow's whistling. She's so relieved that her tune flags, for a second, and the cockatrice's eyelids begin to creep up until she resumes.

A tiny part of her hadn't been sure that it would work. Actually, quite a large part.

She's very glad that part of her was wrong.

Snow shifts the tune slightly, quickening the pace, and the cockatrice's tail lashes out, sending the bandits scattering. Dogtooth yells frantically, but no one is paying attention. They were afraid of the cockatrice before it listened to Snow, and they have no desire to stick around now that Dogtooth's lost his control.

She spots a tiny tunnel on the other side of the cavern.

That's their best bet. The other route might take them out, but they still have all the bandits to contend with, and the logs.

Still whistling, Snow catches Ivan's eye and gestures toward the tunnel.

"Run!" he yells, and the Huntsmen stumble forward on their bound feet. Dimitri's the last one through, and he reaches out and snags her roped wrist, pulling her along with him. Her heart goes frantic at the touch, but it might have to do with the giant monster.

It's hard to run and whistle, the tune going breathy, but she doesn't stop.

The tunnel is narrow, and they're forced single-file, and—

It's a dead end. The chamber is surrounded on all sides by rough, unbroken stone.

"No," Snow whispers.

"Start climbing," Ivan grunts to the Huntsmen.

He's looking up, where light falls through a hole many feet above them. There's no way they can climb up there. At some points, the stone is too smooth for handholds, and even if they did make it, there are so many of them, and it won't take long for the bandits to catch up.

Lucille used to challenge Snow to games of rapid chess, playing with only three seconds' worth of sand in the hourglass for every move. Snow used to crack under the pressure, flinging the chess board to the floor, stomping away, bitter tears spilling as soon as she reached her room.

So she started practicing on her own, one hand on the

hourglass and one on the chess pieces, flipping and moving, flipping and checking, until she learned to think even when time evaporated too fast.

She never imagined that something Lucille taught her would *help* her. Then again, she never imagined Lucille as a centuries-old evil witch, either.

Snow changes the tune again—this time a song of flight, freedom, adventure—and there's a whooshing sound before the cockatrice roars down the tunnel and into the chamber.

"What are you *doing?*" Ivan roars.

Snow takes a gulp of air. "Get on!" she yells, and keeps whistling.

The cockatrice snares the back of her shirt in one claw, Dimitri's in the other, and, out of options, the Huntsmen attach themselves to its back and chain their hands together to link those who aren't able to grab on to the feathers.

Bandits pound into the chamber, and the cockatrice shoots into the air.

Snow glances at Dimitri. He looks awed, staring at the stones rushing by, and soon they're out of the hole, above the cave, soaring through the pine trees.

They're free.

Snow slows the tune, and the cockatrice floats a foot above the ground, unlatching Snow and Dimitri as the other bandits jump off.

Snow scrambles to her feet and finally stops whistling.

Her cheeks hurt. The tune was losing its direction toward the end, but it's over. It's done.

The cockatrice screeches and soars off into the sky.

The Huntsmen gather themselves, taking steadying breaths. A few of them plop onto the ground and cradle their heads between their knees, and the rest get to untying the knots around wrists and ankles, the first ones free hacking at ropes with their daggers.

Then Ivan seizes Snow's arms and tightens the ropes around her wrists.

"All righty, then," he says, clapping his hands. "Not a bad day. Dodged some bandits. And we've still got our princess."

This can't be happening. This hurts worse than the broken wrist. She risked everything to free them because when she was Myrtle, they were so kind to her. But when she is Snow, she is a princess. Not a girl. People seem to forget she needs kindness, too.

"You can't take me back to Lucille," Snow pleads. They still don't believe that she's good, that it's Lucille who's wicked. They don't see who she is. But has anyone, ever? "Everything she said about me . . . it's all a lie. I didn't curse anybody."

"And we're supposed to trust you?" Olive glares at her. "You, who've lied to us since the moment we met? Who cursed those guards asleep?"

"She *saved* us," Dimitri cuts in, making that little flame

glow again inside Snow, but Mud holds him back from going to her.

The Huntsmen exchange glances. Even Ivan looks unsure. But no one intervenes. She may be the rightful heir to the throne, but Lucille is the one who can spin lies like some fairies can spin grain into gold.

Snow whistles for owls, for great horned birds with terrible claws and wingspans as long as a person to rescue her, but whatever magic lives in her is diminished after the cockatrice. Instead, what stream out from the trees look like small feathered croquet balls. They're not going to—

"We're under attack!" Dimitri cries.

Dimitri dives to the ground, shrieking, and his panic captures like a spark in dry grass. The Huntsmen wail, diving into bushes, trying to dig holes in the dirt, the terror from the bandit attack still fresh.

Dimitri catches Snow's eye.

"Run," he mouths.

Snow bolts.

Sooner or later, they'll catch her. The Huntsmen won't stop until they finish their Hunt, she knows, and they'll take her back to Lucille, and she'll lock Snow up so she can't get to the Crown Ceremony. Maybe she'll curse her, too. Snow runs and runs, ignoring the ache in her side and the fire on the bottom of her feet. She's had enough dance lessons to push through pain, and it's nothing like the pain in her chest. How quickly the Huntsmen turned on her.

After everything. For them, it was all about the hunt. Even over hearing the truth.

She runs until she can't run farther.

Snow skids to a halt in front of a river, raging and frothing. It doesn't matter that it's so wide across; even if she dared to venture to its center, she would be swept out by the rapids.

Snow sniffs and wipes her nose on the back of her wrist. Does it matter, how far or how fast she runs? She won't be able to make it back to Apfel.

No. There'll be time to be sad later.

Lucille is counting on her giving up, being afraid, not being clever enough to save herself. Like in every chess game, where Snow has more often than not left the room before it was finished rather than see herself in defeat.

And wanting to prove Lucille wrong is enough to make Snow continue running. She'll . . .

Something crashes behind her, and Dimitri flounders onto the riverbank.

He stops, panting, clutching his knees.

"I didn't think you'd run so fast," he admits.

Snow seizes a branch and wields it against him, wishing she were more advanced in her study of swordplay. But swords always gave her such blisters. Now she realizes how silly those excuses were. She used to do so little, because she was so afraid she'd be bad. Seen as *not enough*. She doesn't want to keep wasting time or knowledge worrying about what other people think about her.

"I'm not here to hurt you," he says hastily.

"Where are they?" Snow demands.

"About ten minutes behind," Dimitri says.

Snow glowers at him. Is it a trick?

But no matter how light-footed the Huntsmen can be, they still make sound, and the woods are quiet except for birds chirping and leaves rustling in the wind.

"Why are you helping me?" Snow asks, still expecting a dagger to the back when she turns.

"Because you . . . you're not what everyone says you are. You almost died to save us. That's not what a curse causer would do. You're a good person, Snow."

Snow hadn't known how desperate she was to hear someone say that. To hear *Dimitri* say that. Her eyes burn, and she blinks quickly. No time to be sad.

"Can you help me get across?" She gestures at the river.

Dimitri frowns. "Oh. Um. No."

They stare at each other.

"I don't know what I'm supposed to do," she whispers.

Dimitri squeezes her hand, like he understands she doesn't mean just now. She means all the moments after she gets back. If she gets back.

"You . . . you just keep going. And you'll figure it out. I know you can."

To keep going, she has to make the Huntsmen give up. The river's banks and shallows are filled with odd, misshapen rocks, some small and smooth, but others lumpy, like mishandled clay. And she wonders . . .

Who among the Huntsmen actually knows what a heart looks like? Hopefully, none.

Snow isn't sure if you can take the heart from someone who's been petrified, but she's not sure the Huntsmen know that, either. At least it buys her time. She wades into the freezing shallows and plucks up a rock about the size of her fist. It could be a heart. She wipes off the wet rock on her dress.

"Tell them that I was petrified," she whispers. "Tell them that the cockatrice came back. Tell them it was angry. And that you took my heart to show Lucille."

"Snow . . ."

"I'm really sorry about your mom," she says.

Dimitri takes the rock from her, testing its weight, his lips puckered. "It's not your fault," he says. "But . . . we need a queen like you. A queen who would risk everything for a few Huntsmen in a cave."

Snow looks down at her shoes. Can she do this? She didn't think she could win at cards, face down bandits, tame a cockatrice. Maybe you can't know what you're capable of until you go out and do it.

"It won't stop them forever." Dimitri cradles the heart-rock. "But it will buy you some time. Run, Snow White."

There's no time to say anything else. In the distance she hears the Huntsmen prowling through the forest.

Once again, Snow runs.

35

Rose

I REALLY THINK YOU SHOULD SEE THIS," YORK insists.

What she needs to do—she needs to scribble a note to Edel. Explain that she knows and understands why Edel never said anything. She's a princess? A cursed one? And the woman who cursed her is in this very castle and now knows there's a second princess wandering around. But there's no possible way she'd assume it's Rose. Rose still isn't convinced it's Rose.

And maybe York really has found something. An answer even the stars didn't see.

"Okay," she agrees.

She stuffs the apple into her bag, just in case it can somehow help her defeat Lucille, and trails York out of the room. Even with the Crown Ceremony tomorrow, the castle is mostly empty. He turns down a hallway she hasn't been in before, up a narrow stairwell that's not familiar.

"Where are we going?" They go up and up and up, farther and farther away from the parts of the castle Rose knows.

York stops at a small room at the top of a tower.

It's dusty. There's an old spinning wheel in the corner, and boxes are shoved against the walls.

"Is this about the notebook?" Rose asks.

"I'm sorry," York says.

"It's okay," Rose says. "Listen, York. There's something you should know."

How do you tell someone you're cursed? That you might be a lost princess?

"I'm sorry," York says again.

"There's nothing to be sorry for." But a strange, bad feeling blooms in her chest. York keeps backing away, and Rose can't move.

At all. She's frozen in place.

Some shade of magic was laid here as a trap.

"She promised that if I helped her, she wouldn't tell my uncle about what happened in the Tombs," York whispers, sounding miserable. "I'm sorry, Rose. I didn't have a choice."

He . . . he tricked her? To save himself from a small embarrassment?

She thought she knew rage when Klaus told her about

the curse, when she realized Edel had kept something this monumental from her for her entire life, but that was nothing compared to this. Because at least that made sense—Edel wanted to protect her. York just wanted to keep out of a little bit of trouble.

"Of course you had a choice!" Rose shouts. "Everyone has choices."

York shakes his head, his eyes red, and then he turns and runs away.

"Coward!" Rose yells.

The door slams behind him, although no one has shoved it.

The invisible bonds holding her in place fall away, but it doesn't matter. The door is locked shut.

"Help!" Rose hollers, hammering her fists against it. *"HELP!"*

But yell as she might, no one answers.

She's trapped.

And alone.

And the clock ticks on toward tomorrow.

36

Snow

SNOW HAS NO IDEA WHERE SHE IS.

> She thinks she's headed east. East-ish. Toward Apfel.

But all she really knows is that she's alone in the center of the Dreamwood.

It starts to rain, and Snow swears, using a few choice words she picked up from the bandits.

Her cloak's in no condition to keep her warm, and it's getting late, and her stomach grumbles, and you shouldn't be in the Dreamwood after dark. A lone girl? The bandits would seem like teddy bears.

The rain picks up. Snow whistles, but no birds come. The whistle sounds too tired and thin.

Shivering, Snow stumbles forward, tilting and flailing

as the path gets increasingly muddy. At least she still has the boots the Huntsmen gave her. Never again is she going to turn down practical footwear.

Even through the rain, Snow can make out shapes drifting among the trees and sounds that make her skin prickle: grunting and sniffling and chittering. Distracted, she trips on something large and barely swallows a scream when she realizes it's just a root.

There. Her eyes land on something that isn't trees or rain.

An entrance is carved into craggy rocks, the cave's mouth littered with what she hopes are animal bones.

It's not the most welcoming place, and there's a sour stench coming from it. But danger lurks without. It doesn't necessarily lurk within.

She ducks into the cave. It seems empty enough. She can see the back, and there's nothing here. Still a risk, but she's desperate. She's exhausted. She's lost.

How did Dimitri think she could do this?

He should have come with her. He should— No. He shouldn't. Because if she gets back to Apfel, what's waiting for her . . . she doesn't think it's going to be good. He doesn't deserve to face that.

Snow slides down the cave wall onto the ground. It's not clean by any stretch of the imagination, but neither is she. The mud all over her body is starting to stiffen and dry.

She can't let her guard down. She has to stay awake, to . . .

37

Snow

THIS MIGHT BE SNOW'S WORST BIRTHDAY.

Usually, she wakes to cinnamon buns richly frosted and caramel hot chocolate. The entire city celebrates, with music and parades throughout the day and fireworks at night. And her father sticks around for once, telling her stories about her mother during the moments he's not chatting up the nobles with the deepest pockets.

On this birthday, she wakes with aching limbs and a kink in her neck, surprised by how much she misses her bed on the Huntsmen's train.

She peeks out the cave's entrance. The storm has cleared. The morning is gray, fog tangled among the trees and ferns.

And she has absolutely no idea how she's supposed to

get home. The Crown Ceremony isn't that far away. Nothing will stop the crown from being placed on Lucille's—the Night Witch's—brow.

There's the sudden sound of a waterfall.

Snow leaps away, looking for the source.

Except there isn't a waterfall.

But there is a man, appearing out of nowhere. He has shockingly silver hair and a shockingly blue suit.

"My, my. Some people have been working very hard to find you," he says.

He beams at Snow, before looking around and gagging in disgust.

"How did *you* find me?" Snow asks.

"I hear the yearning of the pitiful," he declares. "And . . . yuck. You chose to hide in this place? Interesting choice."

"Who are you?" Snow demands. She's not pitiful, thank you very much.

With a dramatic flourish, the man bows. "Durchdenwald, at your service. After everything with my recent celebrity in Miravale, I was expecting a little bit more . . . excitement."

"You're a fairy godfather," Snow realizes. His name's been passed around occasionally at court. Not all wonderful things . . . Still. A fairy godfather. Right now, that's better than nothing.

"Yes, well, of course I am," the man says. "To clarify, I'm not *yours*."

Snow narrows her eyes. "Then why are you here?"

Durchdenwald throws up his arms. "The lack of grati-tude among young ladies today!"

"I'm not really in a place to be grateful for social visits," Snow points out.

He sighs and flings himself across the cave to stand close to Snow.

"Someone asked me to be here," he says. "Someone is concerned about you."

"Concerned about me?" Snow asks.

"Why, of course!" He wriggles his eyebrows at her. "You're Apfel's next queen. You have fans. And they im-plored me to help you. Sorry for the delay. Busy schedule and all that."

This could be a trick.

But what's the worst that could happen? She's already cold, wet, lost, lonely, and very, very far from home.

"You'll help me get back?" she asks.

"Oh. No," he apologizes. "I can see why you would think that. I'm just here to offer an encouraging word. You've got this. Chin up. Et cetera."

Snow blinks. She rode a cockatrice away from bandits. She found a stone heart to trick fairies known for tracking down their quarry against all odds.

And this fairy, with so much magic at his disposal, can only say "chin up"?

Snow is still too drained from the cockatrice to call any more birds. But she has one final weapon.

She tugs the spindle from her pocket, brandishing it at

Durchdenwald as he says, "And I was supposed to make sure someone's told you about that sister business."

"Take me home!" she declares. Then: "*Sister?*"

He jumps back, looking genuinely frightened at the sight of the spindle.

"Are the stories *true?*" he asks. "Are you really causing the curse?"

Snow lowers the spindle.

"Of course I'm not. And what are you— This is for *sewing*," she says.

"It is decidedly not," Durchdenwald declares. For once he looks serious. "I'm a bit concerned that you've been wandering around with that and have no idea what it is."

Snow studies it. It really, really looks like it's for sewing.

"That once belonged to the Night Witch," he says. "It's no wonder it found its way back to you. Objects like that tend to find their owners."

"I'm not its owner," Snow says. The thought of Lucille fills her mouth with bitterness.

"Her blood flows through your veins," Durchdenwald says. "She created that spindle, and she made its prick powerful enough to destroy even her."

Snow wishes she'd known that earlier. Since she's had the spindle, she's mainly avoided touching the point due to luck. "Why would she create something that could hurt *her?*"

"Hunger for power often paves the path to our downfalls," he says. "She created many objects during her reign.

She coaxed the dual apple trees at the castle to grow fruit poisoned with her sleeping curse. She crafted the spindle the same."

"But why would she need that?" The Night Witch was plenty powerful without it.

But Snow isn't. She's relieved—she didn't curse those Miravalian guards. The spindle must have done it.

"To amplify her abilities. At a certain point, the desire for power can no longer be bounded by sense," Durchdenwald says. "And the spindle could do many things. They say it was even how she escaped the Night Garden, and . . . hmm. Perhaps I *can* be more of service to you." He straightens. "Hold the spindle out. *No*. Not in my direction. Point it in the air, and draw a door."

"I . . . I don't think I should," Snow says softly, thinking again of the guards.

Durchdenwald studies her, gentler now. "Oh, child," he says. "You've seen it work, haven't you? You won't hurt either of us now if you focus on your *intention*. Anger and fear cause destruction. Instead, imagine . . . the time you've felt most free."

Snow extends her arm, half-closing her eyes. She imagines . . . flying away from the bandits, the cockatrice soaring them upward, the assuredness that she'd saved her friends and that together they'd save her kingdom. That she'd done something her mother would be proud of. Her chest aches.

Shakily she traces a doorway in the air.

Snow squints. She's no longer staring at the back of the cavern.

She's looking into the Night Garden.

And at its exit, she'll find her castle.

"Wait," Snow says. "You said something about a sister."

"Yes." Durchdenwald flashes his white teeth at her. "Tell Rose hello for me, won't you?"

And he gives her a little nudge, sending her through the doorway.

38

Rose

THIS IS BY FAR ROSE'S WORST BIRTHDAY.
Usually folk from throughout the Dreamwood
come to celebrate, all bearing delicious dishes and
stories and sharing the cakes Edel has baked, one cake for
every year of Rose's life.

But this year, she woke on a pile of burlap sacks, her
eyes watery from all the dust and her throat sore from
hours of yelling for help the day before.

If Lucille, the Night Witch, locked her up, she must
suspect that Rose is the other princess, too. Rose doesn't
want to know what Lucille has planned next.

"Let me out!" Rose resumes banging on the door. She
kicks it, pounds her fists against it. It doesn't open. The

dwarfs don't show up. Apparently, the stars aren't paying attention to her right now.

There's a certain irony to it. She's heard so many stories about trapped princesses, and now here she is, maybe another one of them.

That still sounds too strange. *Princess.*

Rose looks desperately around the chamber for any exit. The door is so firmly shut that it might as well be decoration, and the tower's too high for the window to do any good. There are rumors in the Dreamwood of a girl locked in the tallest tower with only a window to look out at the world beyond, and that's a little how Rose feels right now.

Rose glowers at the spinning wheel. It's missing its spindle. Completely useless. This is a place for abandoned, forgotten things.

And then, though the day feels endless, it passes, without escape, rescue, or food. Rose can hear the sounds of the Crown Ceremony beginning—people chattering, instruments playing. The afternoon light grows golden and heavy.

Surely, surely, *surely,* there must be a solution.

The lock in the door clicks.

Rose's head jerks.

Did she . . . do that? Did she will that? After all, Apfel princesses have magic in their blood.

"You poor, dear thing," Amalia says, shutting the door behind her. "She's got you locked up, hasn't she?"

"Did she send you here?" Rose whispers. She suddenly

wishes she hadn't banged on the door so loud. She's not sure if this is better or worse than being alone.

"Lucille? No. She has no idea I'm here."

Amalia clop-clop-clops across the room. One thin finger pushes Rose's chin up.

"So it is true," she says. "It's in your eyes. I never noticed it before, but . . . it's a dangerous thing, to think there's nothing new for us to see."

Rose shakes her head. Her stomach flips. Amalia thinks it, too. That she's the lost *princess*.

The most ridiculous part is how badly she wants it, even now. To be a princess would mean having a place where she belongs. It would mean the world opening up to her. It would mean family.

"What does she want with me?" Rose whispers.

"You pose a great threat to the Night Witch," Amalia says. She perches on the spinning wheel's seat.

"You know Lucille's the Night Witch?"

A strange look flutters over Amalia's face. "Of course I know. I'm here to help you."

"Help?"

"There is one way to confirm if you are indeed Elora's secret daughter," Amalia says. "And if it works . . . we can stop Lucille from putting on the crown. We can save the kingdom from her wicked plot."

"And the curse?" Rose asks.

"It would be broken. We must get the crown."

"How do you know that?"

"Because you're not the only one trying to ensure that the right queen sits on the throne. It belongs to the bloodline."

Rose gnaws on her lip and glances out the window. The courtyard glimmers with festival lights. It feels like she's missing something. But that could just be from hunger and bafflement.

"What do I have to do?" Rose asks.

"I believe you have an apple with you," Amalia says. "All you need to do is take a bite."

39

Rose

ABITE?" ROSE ASKS.

She pulls the apple out of her pocket. Though it's been sitting on her desk, and now in her dress, for days, it's still as red and firm and sweet-smelling as ever. Up close, there's a metallic undertone. Just like what she smelled in the bakery and on the sleeping nobleman. The smell of the curse.

Amalia nods. "The apple possesses great magic. It will reveal whether you're a descendant of the First Queen."

Apple blossoms can mean "preference." Amalia could be sincere, and Rose would finally know what she's yearned to know her whole life: Who is her family? Where does she belong? Yet the smell of the curse lingers in the air, and what has Amalia done to win Rose's trust? Rose has spent her whole life believing the kindness she's desperate to see in people, and now she's locked up in a tower.

But the curse is coming for her. What does she have to lose?

Still, she points out the window. "When will the Crown Ceremony happen?" she asks.

Amalia glances at the late-afternoon sky. "Soon. We don't have time to waste."

When Amalia isn't looking, Rose slips a rose petal from her belt bag under her tongue.

"Now, girl," Amalia says. "Let's get Apfel her rightful queen."

Rose lifts the apple. There's no other option. Even if this apple is cursed, even if Amalia is lying, this is what has to happen. If she's the cursed princess, she's meant to fall asleep, isn't she? It's Snow who's destined for the throne. She has no time to pity herself.

She presses the apple against her lips. Even the most vicious of plants may help you if you know how to talk to them.

"I want the truth," she whispers, because plants like the truth.

She takes a bite—

40

Snow

SNOW'S NEVER ENTERED THE NIGHT GARDEN. It was considered off-limits even before Lucille arrived and *strictly* forbade Snow from going there.

As much as Snow likes to defy Lucille, when you grow up hearing that your evil many-times-great-aunt filled a garden with lots of nasty things, you keep away.

But the Night Garden isn't what she expected. It reminds her of a painting. The path is nearly like glass. There are thickets of thorns, but they're blooming with huge white flowers that smell sweet, like jasmine.

Snow can't help it. She shivers, even though the Night Witch is long gone and Snow's holding the reason why.

Over there, an exit sign. A few more steps and she'll be home.

Without the Huntsmen. Without an army.

With just a spindle. And a lot of hope.

Snow rushes toward the exit sign.

And vines surge upward from the ground, straight toward her.

41

York

HERE'S WHAT ROSE AND SNOW DON'T SEE.
York, racing up the stairs, clutching his side as
it burns. So angry at himself that it feels like he's
going to explode. He shouldn't have done that to Rose.
But the guards had brought him from the prison to Amalia, where he had stood on her woven Ambrosian carpet,
feeling a bruise from a marble queen forming on his cheek,
and Amalia had tutted, asking what his uncle would think.
Promising he wouldn't know to think anything if York led
Rose into the tower.

And then he spent the night sitting in his empty bath-
tub, shivering, imagining Rose's face as the door slammed
between them.

York's spent most of his life trying to not be himself, to make up for everything he's lacking. Namely, magic.

But since he met Rose, he's realized he doesn't need magic to try to help break a curse. He can still do plenty the way he is.

She's right—he made the wrong choice. But he can still make the right one.

He'll get her out of that tower no matter what, and then . . . then they'll go back to Madame Divine. Or even Lady Grimm. They'll do what they have to in order to break the curse.

And he'll try to find a way to apologize for getting her locked up in a tall, dusty tower.

A pressure clamps the castle, like before a thunderstorm, and York stares out a window.

In the courtyard below, all the guards are sleeping. So are the musicians. So are the horses and the dogs. Even a few pigeons lie on the ground.

All of them look like they've fallen.

York stares, astonished, confused.

"Rose!" he bellows, starting his ascent again.

And then York falls, too.

42

Rose

43

Snow

NOW BACKS AWAY FROM THE VINES,
thrusting the spindle in front of her.

"Get back," she whispers, cursing Durchdenwald. What a terrible rescue job, sending her to be consumed by bramble.

She must be fiercer than she thinks, because the vines
don't come near her. Instead, they grow upward, forming a
kind of table, with a large bloom in the center, big enough
that Snow could crawl inside and be comfortable.

"What are you doing?" she asks the vines, mostly because hearing her voice helps break a silence that makes
her skin prickle.

Gently, the vines drop away. The petals open. In the
center is . . . a girl.

Snow creeps closer. A girl about her age.

Asleep.

And Snow knows her.

She's the girl from the castle, who helped Snow during the panic. She's oddly familiar, with her long strawberry-blond hair, a nice blue dress, a smattering of freckles. A funny little belt bag.

Snow prods the girl.

"Hello?"

The girl doesn't stir.

"Um, wake up?" Snow suggests. She pokes the girl again.

Still nothing.

She's clearly cursed, a stranger caught in the crossfire between Snow and Lucille.

The very least she can do is get this girl somewhere more comfortable. The petals look soft, but they're still on top of thorns.

Carefully, she lifts the girl up.

"Do you see the family resemblance?" someone whispers.

"Who's there?" Snow pauses. She's pretty sure there's no one around except for a lot of plants.

"How lovely to see sisters reunited," the voices whisper.

"Sisters?" Snow yelps, dropping the girl back to the flower.

A bite of apple flies out of her mouth, and the girl's eyes open.

44

Rose

ROSE COUGHS AND COUGHS, LEANING over a table of thorns to spit the sweet taste of the apple and rose petal onto the ground of the Night Garden.

It's loud. Or much louder than it was when she was asleep. Because that was what had happened, she's sure of it. The deepest sleep she's ever felt, a nothingness so big and boundless. Her fingers tingle, and she shakes her arms to wake them up. Was that—it? The curse?

She hopes so. Because that could mean it's over, the Night Witch outsmarted. And she's glad the rose petal worked. It would have been a trickier gamble without it.

Rose always keeps rose petals on hand. Edel says that the flowers we're named after offer special protections.

Rose means "love," and Rose bit the apple out of love. For her family, for Edel, for the people of Apfel, who don't deserve a curse. Even if they'll never know what she's done.

"Welcome back, Princess," the voices in the Night Garden whisper. Another confirmation that makes her stomach squirm.

She asked for the truth, and she got it. She may be a princess, but what's more important now is stopping Lucille.

She leans down, gingerly picking up the apple piece and tucking it into her belt bag.

"Thank you," she whispers, to the rose, to the apple, to the Night Garden.

"You're welcome?" someone says.

"I—" Rose starts. But it's just a girl, not Amalia, not anyone from the castle.

It's just—

That's Snow White.

The princess.

Her . . . her sister.

Snow is streaked with dirt and mud, her dark hair chopped short and greasy, her skin scratched. She's wearing a cloak that's little more than tatters, but there's a fierceness to her. Like you don't want to mess with her.

What do you say to a sister you've only just discovered exists?

"Snow," she begins.

"Who sent you?" Snow demands.

Rose blinks. It's not the reaction she's expecting. "No one."

"You can't take me back to her," she says. Her eyes are a little red, like she's trying not to cry.

"I'm not trying to take you anywhere," Rose says. "What happened to you? Everyone was wondering where you were."

"Because everyone thinks I caused the curse," Snow says bitterly.

"Of course you didn't," Rose says. "Lucille did."

Snow grits her teeth. "I know. But . . . wait. What were you doing in that flower?"

That's the kind of long story they don't have time for. With each of Rose's heartbeats, she hears the ticking of the clock.

"This is going to sound strange," Rose says. "But I think . . . I think I'm your sister."

"So I've been told. You're Rose?" Snow asks. She puffs out her cheeks and tilts her head. "Are you the reason I can't sing?"

"Am I—what?"

"When I was born, a fairy gave me the gift of a beautiful singing voice. I don't have that. Can you sing?"

Rose nods. She can sing fine. It's never been anything she thought about.

"Are you bad at lying?"

Rose nods again.

"That makes sense," Snow says. She paces back and forth, avoiding the vines. The cloak tatters flop at her back. "Because I didn't really get the gift of honesty, either."

"If it helps," Rose says, "you have much better posture than I do."

Snow stares at her.

And then they both burst out laughing. Rose isn't sure why, only that everything has been so much, so unbelievable.

Snow stops giggling first. "I'm sorry that you got pulled into this. An evil witch. A battle for a throne."

"I don't want it. Your throne," Rose promises. After all, there's only ever been one princess of Apfel, one queen of Apfel. So what if Rose is a queen's daughter? Nothing will change.

"Enough people do," Snow says, looking relieved. "I don't think I could handle another one."

Rose has so many questions: Will she and Snow be friends after this? Will the king—her father—want to meet her? Could this help her get into the RAA? Does she even still want to go to the RAA? She's not who she thought she was, so who does that mean she is?

First, though, they have a curse to break.

Rose quickly fills Snow in on the contract, Elora's notebook, the mirror, the apple.

"Right now, Lucille and Amalia think I'm asleep. And they think you're missing," she says.

"Neither of them is looking for us," Snow agrees. She

tugs a spindle out of her pocket. "They think they've won. But we have this."

She explains what Durchdenwald said. Another advantage the Night Witch doesn't know about.

Snow taps her bottom lip, thinking. "If the crown is placed on Lucille's head, it'll give her its power."

Neither of them seems to want to add: *more power than she already has.*

If she's capable of cursing a city without the crown, what is she capable of *with* it?

"We need to get you to the throne room," Rose says. "Before Lucille."

45

Dimitri

THE TWO SISTERS DON'T SEE THIS, EITHER.
Dimitri staggers up to the castle of Apfel, panting
and muddied, his face screwed up with determina-
tion. His shirt is ripped from the bandits and ruined from
the run through the rain and his journey to get here, after
taming a wild griffin to fly him through the night.

Snow shouldn't have to face down her wicked stepmother alone.

All will be well. The prince of the Huntsmen comes to
the rescue.

But that's not how this story goes.

Magic ripples outward, and Dimitri falls, too.

46

Snow

IT DOESN'T SOUND LIKE SUCH A HARD TASK, getting to the throne room, but as soon as they step out of the Night Garden, Snow falters. Rose gasps.

It's . . . everyone is . . .

Asleep.

Servants snore on the windows they were cleaning, on the tables they were dusting, on the velvet-lined trays of silverware they were polishing. Even the fleas have stopped jumping, the spiders stopped weaving.

In the main courtyard, nobles lie on the tables, frosting from cakes smeared in their hair. Snow hears Rose's stomach rumble at the sight of the food, and hers does the same.

Ambassadors are half in the koi ponds. Guards snooze between flowers. Quite a few people showed up for her

Crown Ceremony, even with the curse. Snow's flattered. But Lucille's—the Night Witch's—power has seized them all.

"I guess the curse is here," Rose whispers. She keeps pinching her inner arm like she's trying to make sure she's awake.

Snow never thought about a sister. It was hard enough getting her father's attention without imagining *sharing* it. But it's kind of nice having Rose around, someone who's been equally impacted by this, who understands what all of this is like. "Throne room," Snow says.

"Throne room," Rose agrees.

And fast. They run alongside each other, through the silent halls, the silent corridors, dodging cats lying asleep, servants stretched out with shattered goblets beside them, nobles snoring, and merchants clutching their order forms.

Lucille did this? Snow feels furious all over again. Lucille is willing to destroy a kingdom so long as she can claim it. And she robbed Snow of the chance to have a real stepmother. To have a family that felt like a family.

They pause at the throne room's large doors. Rose squeezes Snow's hand quickly, and Snow feels a little less alone.

"I think all you have to do is put on the crown," Rose whispers. "That'll stop this. I'm sure of it."

Snow grips the door handle. What if they've gotten it all wrong? What if the crown does nothing? What then?

Clop-clop-clop.

The girls spin around.

"What a relief," Amalia says. "You two found each other."

47

Rose

NO." ROSE BACKS UP. "YOU TRIED TO *poison* me."

"I was testing you," Amalia corrects. She shuffles toward her. "To ensure you were fair of heart. Only a true daughter of Apfel could wake up from such a strong curse."

Snow tenses. "She's lying, Rose."

"Am I?" Amalia asks. "Or am I helping? My loyalty has always been to the kingdom of Apfel. I won't let Lucille take it."

Rose isn't sure who she trusts; Amalia gave her the apple, but because of that, Rose is now awake to help Snow. They can't discount potential allies. Still, Rose has learned how easy it is for people to make the wrong decisions.

"The kingdom is in danger," Amalia warns. "Get the crown before Lucille comes, Snow White."

"I'd rather you didn't."

Lucille strides down the hallway. For the Crown Ceremony, she wears a shimmering dress that reminds Rose of a snake that has slithered through molten gold. Her blond hair flows loose around her shoulders, her lips painted a fiery red.

She doesn't look like a Night Witch. Which is probably why she chose this as a disguise.

"Enter the throne room, girls," Amalia says. Rose's head swivels between them. Snow glares at Lucille like she's never hated anyone more.

"How dare you," Snow spits out at Lucille.

"*Don't* go through that door," Lucille snarls.

"We have to do something!" Snow cries. Taking Rose's forearm, she charges into the throne room, Amalia clop-clop-clopping behind them. They run toward the pedestal, the glimmering crown. It looks so innocent and beautiful.

"Do *not* touch that crown," Lucille sings. "I'm still the queen consort. You have to listen to me."

"Go," Amalia hisses, shoving Rose. "Grab it."

Rose stumbles forward, but then the floor heaves, throwing her and Snow to the ground.

A wild wind sweeps around them. Thunder crackles in the throne room, temporarily deafening Rose. Ancient dust long forgotten is whipped at them, forcing Rose to screw her eyes shut.

When she opens them again, Lucille is no more.

Amalia snarls.

Something much bigger snarls back.

A massive dragon as black as night, with wings as big as dread and a swishing spiked tail, glares at them with golden eyes.

48

Snow

YOU HAVE GOT TO BE KIDDING.

Lucille, a *dragon?*

No one ever mentioned that the Night Witch could turn into a dragon.

If only they had. That might have changed Snow's approach.

Actually, if only her father had *thought a little more carefully* before getting married. Shouldn't the barristers have poked around into Lucille's past a little better before allowing her to marry *a king?*

"Oh-ho," Amalia mutters. "I didn't know you had that in you, Lucille."

Rose hurries over to Snow, then pulls her up and dives

behind the two apple trees as a blast of heat sears their backs.

"Watch out!" Rose gasps, patting down a glowing ember on her cloak. "She *breathed fire* at us!"

Snow gasps, peeking back.

Dragon Lucille makes the cockatrice look puny. With a horrific shattering sound, she flexes her wings, sending wood flying from the ceiling, crumbling priceless wall carvings, setting one of the chandeliers swaying dangerously before it plummets to the ground. She bares her huge pointed teeth and opens her mouth: fire crackles along the throne room floor, although the apple trees stand unmarked.

Snow's heart quakes. The flames fill the room with smoke and heat, and Snow feels scared and small and determined. She won't let Lucille get away with this, but she's really not sure they can stop her.

Rose, coughing from the smoke, digs through her belt bag.

"I don't have anything in here that will help with a dragon," she moans. "Maybe if we could find some mint, or, better yet, snapdragon . . ."

"I don't think that's going to happen," Snow says.

Dragon Lucille bellows, and the room shakes. Her tail lashes out. She exhales another stream of fire, and the throne ignites.

Snow gasps. She rarely comes to this room. It reminds her of how unready she feels to be queen, to sit on that throne and make decisions with such great consequences. But to sit there had been one more connection to her mother, one of the very few things they would ever be able to share.

"Grab the crown! End this!" Amalia shrieks, huddling in a corner near the crown's pedestal, despite the blaze.

Snow still doesn't trust Amalia, but she's pretty sure Amalia is right.

"Go!" Rose urges. "I'll distract her."

Snow has no idea how that will work, but she sprints toward the throne. The crown shimmers. She's thought about it so much, but it always surprises her how small it is. Thin, delicate, the two pearls gleaming.

Snow's hands drift forward just as Rose screams.

The dragon has plucked her up with claws that end in points as sharp as a thorn.

Snow didn't expect a sister, but she feels a fierce protectiveness for her now.

"Let her go!" Snow cries. She yanks the spindle out of her pocket, waving it at Lucille.

She really doesn't believe it's going to do much good against those scales, and there's no way she could get close enough to try.

But the dragon recoils.

Amalia laughs. "Well," she says. "Look what always makes its way back."

She plucks the spindle from Snow's surprised grasp. "Where did you find this?" Before Snow can respond,

Amalia smiles a horrible smile. "I knew I couldn't trust those thugs to keep it hidden properly. But it worked out in the end, didn't it? Now we have ourselves a little help."

Amalia traces a hole in the air, revealing the Night Garden.

It feels like someone is gripping Snow's heart and squeezing hard.

Only those related to the Night Witch are supposed to be able to use that spindle. And Snow and Rose are the only ones alive who are related to her.

Along with the Night Witch herself.

Amalia whispers something under her breath, and instead of entering the Night Garden . . . the Night Garden comes to them.

Vines, twisted and massive and thorned, burst through the holes, ripping outward and multiplying with a force that sends Snow reeling. They form a dome over Amalia and Snow, forcing Dragon Lucille away. She drops Rose, who cries out and scrambles toward Snow, a gash ripping in her dress as she crawls under the thorns.

The vines tear holes through the sides of the throne room, racing up high and smashing the half-dome ceiling. Snow covers her head to block the glass shards raining down on her.

"How did you do that?" Snow breathes.

"How hard is it for you to listen to an order, child?" Amalia barks. "Grab. The. Crown. *This kingdom needs its rightful queen!*"

The dragon growls, and flames shoot among the thorns. Some of the vines blacken and wither, but none of them give way.

"You don't mean me, do you?" Snow whispers. "Or Rose?"

"You're finally catching on," Amalia says.

She lunges forward. Snow skids out of the way, so Amalia aims for Rose, seizing her arm.

Amalia grabs Rose tight, hovering her spindle at the girl's neck.

Rose stares at Snow, terrified. The dragon growls, pacing outside the thorns, but doesn't attack.

"Like I said, Princess," Amalia drawls. "Grab the crown."

49

Rose

ROSE TRIES NOT TO TREMBLE, IN CASE SHE accidentally hits her neck against the spindle.

"Grab the crown," Amalia repeats.

Rose suspected but couldn't believe it. Amalia, the Night Witch. It makes sense. Amalia handed her the cloak with the silver. The mirror said she had just looked at the Night Witch, right after Amalia had passed her. Amalia wanted her to eat the apple.

And those horrible, loud shoes! The Night Witch was forced to wear iron shoes that burned her feet.

She needs Rose or Snow to grab the crown. And once she has it . . .

"Was it you?" Rose whispers. "With the almonds?"

Amalia turns to her. "You are quite clever," she says. "You do remind me so much of me."

Snow still hasn't moved, looking between Rose and Amalia, horrified. Just beyond the vines, fire crackles. The dragon swishes its tail. The thorns on the vines seem to be getting bigger.

"You?" Snow stammers. "You . . . you can't be the Night Witch."

Amalia looks disgusted. "You always were a useless little brat," she spits. "Years, decades, centuries, I watched the descendants of my blood fail to bring Apfel to its glory. Weak, all of them. Gutless maggots. Like my sister. Like your *mother,* who wanted you so badly she would risk an entire kingdom."

"So Lucille was helping *you?*" Snow's voice trembles.

Rose can't imagine how Snow feels. Everything she thought, wrong. Everyone around her, plotting.

"Lucille?" Amalia tosses her head back and laughs. "Speaking of gutless maggots!"

Lucille screeches; her massive spike-covered tail swings toward the vines, shattering some of them, but the dome doesn't break.

"You tried to kill me," Rose whispers, thinking of the cloak in the Night Garden.

"Oh, silly girl!" Amalia looks at her. There's . . . kinship in her eye, but it's twisted, evil, rotten. "Never kill. I thought you were just a silly little peasant, sticking her nose where she didn't belong. I just wanted to . . . temporarily take you out of the equation. But after you found Elora's notebook and survived the apple . . . I realized who you were. And I'm impressed."

Why isn't Lucille breathing fire, reducing them all to ash?

It's almost as if . . .

As if Lucille doesn't want to hurt them.

"So impressed," Amalia murmurs, "that I began to wonder if perhaps there was hope for my bloodline yet."

Rose thinks they may have gotten all of this wrong.

"I'll get the crown," Rose says.

It's like another curse has fallen over the room, how still it suddenly becomes.

"What?" Snow whispers.

Amalia *needs* her. She doesn't know how Amalia was planning to get the crown without them, but she doesn't think it was going to be nice.

The dragon growls.

"Rose." Amalia sounds pleased.

"If she gets the crown," Rose says, nodding toward Snow, "they're just going to send me away, aren't they?"

Amalia nods. She lowers the spindle.

"Don't forget how my own sister treated me. This will never be yours," Amalia says. "If you help me, though, I'll reward you, Rose. The Night Garden listens to you, doesn't it? All plants do, don't they? Because magic flows through your veins, same as mine. I'll teach you how to wield it."

And isn't this in some way what Rose *has* always wanted? Someone who sees her, some family member who understands her? Who will help her master what she can do?

"Don't you want to know about the apple?" Amalia asks. "How to make plants bend to your will, become what you need them to be?"

"Don't listen to her," Snow whispers.

Rose's heart thuds. Like Amalia can hear it, she opens her arms. Rose's aunt. Great-great-a-thousand-times-great-aunt.

"No," Snow gasps.

"Imagine having power," Amalia whispers. "The power to never be at anyone's mercy ever again."

Rose steps toward her.

"That's not power," Rose whispers. "That's not how a queen should think."

From her belt bag, she grabs the piece of poisoned apple and shoves it into Amalia's mouth.

50

Snow

AMALIA'S EYES TURN BLACK, HER BODY sags, and the vines around them twist and writhe, furious, going after the girls. The spindle tumbles out of Amalia's grip, rolling harmlessly around the floor.

Dragon Lucille blasts a stream of fire. Finally, it catches on the vines, flames running up and down the stalks, turning the leaves to ash, but the flames dance, uncontrolled, surging toward Snow and Rose. Snow can feel the heat prickle the back of her arms.

"Get the crown!" Rose cries, stepping away from where Amalia lies inert on the floor. "Try and stop this!"

Snow seizes the crown.

It's light and cold. It seems unbelievably harmless.

If she puts it on, she'll finally get to see her mother.

Hear her say that she's proud of her.

Hear her say that she believes in her.

Hear her say that she loves her.

Rose yelps as the fire begins to spread, leaping off the vines and onto the ground.

This crown—Snow's mother was willing to risk this just to have her. And Rose.

And she never got to meet them.

This crown is everything Snow's supposed to want.

And it's everything everyone else wants, too, spawning centuries of wars and curses and betrayals.

Snow takes a deep breath and drives the spindle between the crown's two pearls.

51

Rose

THE CASTLE—MAYBE EVEN THE WORLD itself—shudders so furiously that Rose falls to her knees.

Something soft strokes her cheek.

It's . . . petals.

Ruby-red rose petals, floating around them as the vines dissolve into the air. The fires are nothing but disappearing streams of smoke.

Through the holes in the ceiling, moonlight shines down. A few flakes of late-fall snow pirouette, mingling with the petals to land on the ravaged throne room. Chunks of wood lie everywhere. Burn marks streak up and down the walls. The throne is just splinters.

Rose reaches her hands out, catching a few snowflakes. They're bracingly cold.

Snow stands a few feet away, her mouth open and her eyes wide.

The crown is still clenched in her fist, but the spindle has done its work. It's less a crown and more a mangled, burnt-looking piece of metal, and when Snow tosses it to the ground, it disintegrates into gold-colored ash.

Both girls stare as the ash is whisked upward, and gone.

The only thorns that remain—a dome-shaped knot holding Amalia in place. She appears to be asleep.

Rose's entire body feels unsteady, like she's just gotten back to solid land after years at sea.

Snow turns to her.

"So," Snow says softly, "how do you like it so far, being a princess?"

Rose laughs shakily.

The Night Witch is vanquished. Apfel must be safe. The curse must be over.

But still. She is not *the* princess. After this she'll go back home. To the Wood. Snow will be someone she hears about in stories. Maybe once in a while they'll exchange letters. Will her father keep missing her? Did he ever?

"Hmm." A woman shakes herself out of the debris, straightening her golden skirts. "That was not what I expected at all."

52

Snow

EXCEPT FOR A BURNING GLEAM IN HER EYES, there is nearly no trace that Lucille was, moments ago, a dragon nearly as large as the throne room itself.

Snow backpedals, grabbing Rose and pulling her with her. They nearly smack into the two apple trees, which are unharmed from the battle and now frothing with red and white blossoms.

Amalia might be asleep. But just because Lucille isn't the Night Witch doesn't mean she's not a threat.

"Oh, girls. I do owe you an apology. I should have caught on to Amalia earlier," she says, flicking rose petals off her sleeve. "But I was a bit distracted trying to track you down, Snow. I'm afraid I wasn't a very good fairy god-mother at the end."

Fairy godmother?

"You can't keep lying to me," Snow says.

Lucille holds up her hands, which doesn't seem to signify much, considering she doesn't need to hold a weapon to do damage.

"I promise. No more tricks," she says. "I understand if you don't believe me, Snow. But it's the way it had to be. After what happened at your birth, with Amalia, Edel took Rose away so she could be raised safe, and in secret. And your mother called on me to watch you. I did it without your knowledge for many years, but once rumors spread in the Dreamwood of the Night Witch's return, I knew I needed to be closer."

"Yeah, right," Snow snorts. "You just wanted to be queen."

Lucille makes a face. "You saw what I can become, Snow. You think I'm so desperate for power, I'd willingly go into politics?"

That . . . actually is a good point. In some ways, being a dragon does sound better than being a princess.

But. "You *locked me in my bedroom.*"

"Delegates from Miravale were coming, and I was concerned that one of them might be the Night Witch in disguise."

"You . . . you took my pastries!"

"Out of an overabundance of caution over a poisoning."

"You pushed me through a mirror."

"Amalia pushed you through a mirror. I had no idea what had happened to you."

"You hired the Huntsmen to track me down!"

"To get you safely home. I was even desperate enough to resort to Durchdenwald," she says patiently. "Those awful rumors Amalia spread didn't help get you back. That's when I started to suspect she was behind it."

"Was it you?" Rose asks. "Who brought me here?"

Lucille shakes her head. "It was likely the mirror. There is a balance required with magic, especially magic that strong. To keep that balance, when one princess was forced away, it brought another back. I recognized you the moment you walked into that throne room. I knew you would have a role in breaking the curse, but more than anything, I wanted to keep you close. As safe as possible." She arches an eyebrow. "Perhaps there was room for improvement."

"The apple?" Rose asks.

"I thought it could come in handy," Lucille says. "Luckily, I got that right."

"There's no way that you're my fairy godmother," Snow accuses.

"I understand why you do not like me, Snow," Lucille says, sounding slightly hurt. "I had a role to play, and it was not a kind one. The Night Witch was plotting her return, and she was more likely to drop her guard if she took me for someone wrapped up in my own desperation to be queen. When people think they are at their most powerful, they can be their most vulnerable."

"You played that role really well," Snow shoots back.

"I'm not proud of it," Lucille says softly. "And do not think that I did not grow to care for you."

Snow can't believe it. Lucille has been so awful to her. Although . . . she made sure the cooks wrote down Snow's mother's favorite recipes. She taught Snow chess and made her wake up early for physical training. Whenever Snow finished a book, there was always a new one on her nightstand. And . . . didn't it help? She could think under pressure. She could keep running.

She always thought those were taunts. But a story can become an entirely different one if you look at it from a new perspective. All that's wicked can become good. The lonely princess . . . turns out not to have been so alone after all.

"Did my father know?" Snow asks softly.

Lucille shakes her head. "Marius had no idea. He believed our marriage was one of convenience only, to make the ministers happy. Elora kept the curse a secret from him."

Did Lucille feel lonely, too? Snow desperately wanted to get along with her but was mean and cold, building a rough shell out of fear that Lucille might not like her.

"My job is done here, then," Lucille says. "Good luck, little princesses." Lucille places her hand on Snow's shoulder.

"You're leaving?" Snow asks, her voice cracking. If all along Lucille was something like a mother, she doesn't want to lose her, too.

"I'll be back when you need me most. And when you tell my story, do try and be kind. I know how they love to portray the wicked old stepmother."

The throne room beams with light, as though the sun has tumbled through the thorns and landed at their feet.

Snow reels back, her arm thrown over her eyes, and when the light finally fades, the throne room is empty.

"She's gone," Rose marvels, which is a bit obvious.

"It's over," Snow says, which is also a bit obvious, but saying it helps it feel real.

It's over.

The two princesses step out of the throne room. The vines spread throughout the castle: holes splinter through walls, gardens are ripped up at the root, tiled pathways are demolished.

But that can all be fixed.

A bird starts to sing. A cat meows.

Slowly, the people lying on the ground begin to stir.

53

Snow

S NOW STANDS IN FRONT OF THE MIRROR,
Newton perched on her shoulder. She strokes his
silky head.

It's not the mirror she's supposed to be standing in
front of, which is a few floors above and surrounded by a
team of hairstylists and cosmeticians and the dressmaker,
who are all expecting Snow to waltz in and be beautified
after her time with the healers. Just in time for the Crown
Ceremony, without the actual crown. Her father wrote
that Edel had made a coronet out of flowers until a new
crown could be forged.

"Well, well," the mirror in the cellar says. "I thought
you would be back."

The mirror that started this whole mess.

For the last two days, Snow has mostly been in her bedroom, tended to by healers. But she feels fine, if a bit in shock. At night she'll lie awake, thinking she sees the shadow of giant dragon wings fall over the stars. And when she can't sleep, she creeps over to Rose's room, where they curl up in bed together and whisper stories about their lives, making up for lost time. Part of Snow wishes Lucille were with them; she misses what they could have had.

From Snow's window, she can see the repair work begin on the castle, which is once again bustling. Even if some people are afraid of lingering traces of the curse, more are thrilled to see where the great battle took place. A few have started giving tours.

Amalia, she's told, is being held within the most secure prison in Reverie, deep below the ground, sleeping.

"What do you want to know?" the mirror says now. "You don't even have to do the whole *mirror, mirror* spiel."

"Will I . . ." Snow trails off.

She was going to ask if she will be a good queen. But a mirror can't tell her that. She has to figure that out for herself.

"Would she have been proud of me?" Snow asks instead, her voice small.

"Oh," the mirror says, sounding almost sad. "Of course, Snow White. Every day Elora was pregnant with you and your sister, she would come to me and ask if you were healthy. She loved you from the beginning." Snow feels a funny combination of happy and longing. To think her mother had stood like she is. The invisible things she passed on. "There are many questions you will face while growing up, but that should never be one of them. Now. You've got company."

Snow spins, sparking with dread, almost expecting a wrathful and awake Amalia, but instead she's swept into a hug by Dimitri.

It's strange, seeing him here, but warmth rushes through her. She didn't know if they'd ever meet again.

Ivan, Olive, and Mud follow behind.

"How did you find me?" Snow asks.

"We're good at finding things," Olive says. "Believe it or not."

"They wouldn't let us see you for *days*," Dimitri says. "We tried."

"Lucille is gone," Snow says. "I don't think you're supposed to try to capture me anymore."

"We're here to apologize," Ivan says. "For the whole hunting business."

He pauses, glances at the mirror, which has fallen silent.

"I knew your mother," he adds. "She hired me for a hunt, to find someone who could help her have a baby. Amalia. I didn't know. But . . . If I had never . . ."

If he had never, then none of this would have happened. Snow wouldn't be here. Neither would Rose. We can't know how our decisions are going to shape the world.

"It's okay," she says. "It's just good to see you."

All four of them envelop her in a hug. They accept her

as Snow. She didn't realize how desperately she needed that.

Snow pulls away first.

"Do you still want to be friends?" Snow asks Dimitri. "Now that you know I'm a princess?"

Dimitri grins. "I'll consider it," he says. "And besides, you're not really a princess anymore. You're almost a queen."

54

Rose

N O ONE SEEMS SURE WHAT TO DO WITH
Rose. Like Snow, she's kept under the healers'
care for two days in her castle bedroom, her only
hints of what's happening beyond the doors snippets of
news from the healers. They make her drink water with
salt and lemon and sip a tonic of chamomile and echinacea
for healing. Someone keeps slipping her orange rolls, and
she suspects it's one of the healers who takes pity on her
for her diet of bland oat cakes.

A rotation of healers is around nearly all the time. An
alchemist elder studies her, to see if any of the curse from
the apple remains.

Finally, when Rose hasn't dropped into spontaneous

sleep again, they clear her. The Crown Ceremony will happen that night, they remind her, as if she could forget.

"You have a visitor," one of the healers says, bustling about the end of her bed, where Rose lounges, flipping through a book.

"Who?" Rose asks, surprised. Snow usually comes by later.

"You can't be mad at someone holding orange rolls," York says, entering with a plate in front of him.

As it turns out, she *can* still be mad. *"You."*

"I came as soon as I could," York says. He places the rolls at the desk and then steps back. The bruise on his cheek is fading. "They wouldn't let me in. Or let me send letters. It was to help you rest. I don't know. But anyway. The orange rolls got past them."

"She tried to *curse* me." Rose swings herself out of bed, glaring at him.

"I tried to come get you," he says hurriedly. "I went up to the tower and everything, but then the curse happened. And then I woke up. And everything was fixed. The point is . . . I'm sorry, Rose. I'm really sorry. I don't want us to stop being friends. I liked trying to break curses with you."

She liked it, too. And she understands why he did what he did, a little.

Because when she was lying to Amalia to get her to drop her guard, there was a moment when she thought it would be so, so easy to not be lying. To take the power Amalia promised. To make the wrong choice.

"Maybe we should try it again sometime," Rose says, but a little sadly. York's life is here. And hers . . .

"Another visitor," a healer announces. "In the garden."

"Go," York says. "I'll wait with the rolls, and I won't even have one until you get back."

"You're allowed to eat," Rose says.

"I keep having to apologize to you," he admits, which Rose is aware of. "So I'm going to do every nice thing I can possibly think of."

Rose kisses him on the cheek, blushing and hurrying behind the healer to the garden. If she could stay here, with Snow, York, the RAA . . . No. She can't get her hopes up.

Edel waits at a spindly little table with Rose's favorite lemon loaf in front of her. The guards eye Edel with a bit of fear. She looks exceptionally out of place among the ornate, trimmed rosebushes: soil on her elbows, what appears to be blackberry jam streaked on her apron.

Rose rushes toward her, and Edel rises to let her collapse into her arms. She smells like home: like baking bread, like herbs and crushed flowers.

"Oh, look at you, Rosie," Edel murmurs. "I tried to get here sooner, but . . . a story for another time. What an adventure you've had."

And now it's over. Rose has been dreading this. She loves Edel, she loves home, so . . . how can you love a place but still want something else?

"When are we leaving?" Rose asks.

Edel cocks her head. "Leaving, love?"

"For the Wood."

Edel busies herself cutting off a slice of the lemon loaf. Its scent is tart and sweet.

"I'll leave after the ceremony," Edel says, and Rose is relieved.

"So I can stay a little bit longer?" she asks.

Edel slides the plate of lemon loaf to Rose. "You wouldn't believe how many gifts came for your birthday, especially after the news."

The news that she's a princess.

It still feels absolutely ridiculous, like a pair of boots five sizes too big.

"Have you told the, um, the king?" Rose can't quite get herself to say "my father."

"The king knows, yes," Edel says. "He's held up in the northern provinces, addressing remaining concerns over the curse."

So that's why the king hasn't come to see Rose. And York said no letters were delivered to her for the past two days. Maybe he *did* send a message to her. Rose thought she didn't hear from the king—her father—because he simply didn't care.

"There were, in fact, quite a number of people involved in this decision." Edel purses her lips.

"What decision?" Rose asks.

"It's a bit unprecedented, after all, for Apfel to have two queens."

"Well, two princesses," Rose clarifies. "Snow will be queen."

"As will you." Edel's eyes are watery. "You both will be training to take the throne. Together."

Rose blinks. "But . . ."

The woodcutter's cottage is her home. She may have a father and a sister now, but Edel is her mother.

"The First Queen and her sister built this city to rule together. It has always wanted two queens. It just never had the right ones."

"I don't . . ."

"This isn't goodbye." Edel pinches her cheeks. "I'll be visiting, Rosie dear. Don't you worry."

A vision floods through Rose: waking up in her castle bedroom, hurrying between RAA classes, dining with her sister and her father, brewing potions, running around the city with York, hearing stories about a mother she never knew.

Edel takes Rose's hands and presses them between her own. "I'm afraid part of growing up is leaving some of the things we love. It won't always be easy, Rosie. But you've proven yourself more than ready for what lies ahead."

"Edel . . ." It's hard for Rose to speak. She wants this new life so badly, just as it makes her heart break a little to know that the life she had with Edel is ending.

"And make me proud at the RAA, won't you? Show them what real potion-making is all about."

55

Snow & Rose

THE TWO SISTERS STAND BY ONE OF THE
castle's windows. Outside, everyone waits: the dwarfs,
with their caps clutched to their chests; the Huntsmen; Dimitri; York; someone in a bright blue suit that looks
suspiciously fairylike; Prince Amir and his family; the recently enlarged Villeneuve Trading Company family, who
were always so kind to Rose; warlock clans; the Ironhall Bandits, pacified after a new treaty; and crowds and crowds of
people from across Reverie.

When the sun slants in a certain way, it looks like there's
a woman with golden hair and a dragon tattoo, but then a
cloud shifts, and she's gone.

When the sisters walk out, they'll find the king of Apfel
and Edel before the throne room, with two new crowns

made out of rose vines and apple blossoms from the throne room trees, one for each princess.

The two sisters grasp each other's hands.

And they all lived—

Well. Let's not get ahead of ourselves, shall we?

Acknowledgments

Some books spill onto the page as if they burst into your mind fully formed. Others take a bit (a lot) more coercing. This book fell into the second category.

Don't tell the fairy-tale committee, but it was likely because Snow White and Sleeping Beauty were among my least favorite characters when I was growing up. (I said don't tell the fairy-tale committee!) I didn't like the idea of girls sleeping through more than half the story. I spent most of my free time reimagining *The Hobbit* with a female protagonist who befriended Smaug, saved Bilbo, and looked suspiciously like me.

But once I started getting to know these versions of Snow and Rose, I was reminded about the magic of fairy tales (and the magic of writing them). They can be told and retold, our imaginations weaving around stories we know so well as we wonder, What if nothing is quite like it seems? What if wickedness and goodness are a little harder to tell apart? What if the things we expect just . . . switch? As a writer, there's nothing more exciting than discovering where those questions take you.

This book would not exist without the wonderful team at Random House Children's Books, in particular my brilliant and kind cheerleader/editor, Tricia Lin. Tricia, the world of Reverie and the people who live there become richer and more fascinating with every note and conversation we share. I am so grateful to partner with you on this series. Thanks also to Caroline Abbey, Mallory Loehr, Michelle Cunningham, Michelle Canoni, Rebecca Vitkus, Clare Perret, Alison Kolani, Tracy Heydweiller, David Gilmore, Erica Stone, and Lena Reilly.

Laurel Symonds, I'm excited for this adventure—and many more—with you. Hilary Harwell, thank you for your enthusiasm for these books and all the others. And to everyone at KT Literary, thanks for helping bring so many beautiful books into the world.

I started writing stories in first grade, and that passion was encouraged by incredible teachers in my early education, specifically Diane Parham, Malia Greening, and Eric Ensey. Against the odds and across the decades, your kindness and affirmations kept me returning to the page. There are few things more vital than a good teacher.

With acknowledgments, I always feel like I'm leaving

people out. If you're reading this and wondering if your name is going to appear, it probably belongs here. Thank you, thank you, and I'm sending you lots of love.

Aidan, this book is built off the coffee, Thai food, late-night support, and belief in me that you offer in abundance. Life's more vivid and wonderful with you around.

Mom, Dad, Jen—your support over the years has been instrumental in giving me the confidence to pursue a career as a writer and to take big risks in where I'm living or what I'm doing. Tyler, I sincerely hope the fact that your sister has written books makes me a little cooler in your eyes, even though I know nothing about sports.

Lastly, and once again, thank you, reader. I dreamed a long time about writing stories that would end up in hands like yours. I hope these books can help inspire you to chase after your dreams, too.